ALSO BY BRIAN DRAKE

JACK SLAYTON

October Blood

SAM RAVEN

Terminal Memory

Wicked City

Lady Death

The War Business

The Kill Fever

No Name on my Grave

Bullet Alley

Vengeance Strike

London Assault

Blood Mist

The Murder Mind

The Dark Passage

IRON GHOST

JACK SLAYTON

BOOK 2

BRIAN DRAKE

ROUGH
EDGES
PRESS

Iron Ghost
Paperback Edition

Rough Edges Press
An Imprint of Wolfpack Publishing
1707 E. Diana Street
Tampa, FL 33610

roughedgespress.com

Paperback ISBN 978-1-68549-657-9
Ebook ISBN 978-1-68549-459-9
LCCN 2026938388

IRON GHOST

PROLOGUE

THE PAST

IF COMMANDER JACK SLAYTON HADN'T GONE FOR HIS CIGARETTES, he'd have died with the others.

The Shipwreck Bar. Coronado, CA. Hangout for Navy SEALs and wannabes who followed in their wake. Great place to meet chicks, too—like the SEAL Bunnies all the single team members messed with more than they probably should have. There was always an eager batch of new SEAL groupies to pick from, and the younger members of the team always fell into the trap. It was the older shooters like Slayton who knew better from bad experiences in the past.

Slayton and five others from his unit drove over from the base after a long day of dive training. They were six beers deep when Chief Petty Officer Hank Downing wanted to get out of the noise and go smoke. Downing preferred flavored cigarillos, and Slayton refused his offer to share.

Slayton wanted his Marlboros, but he'd left them in the pickup.

Slayton pushed open the heavy oak door and crossed three rows of cars in the parking lot. The only space available to him on arrival was where the lot met the sidewalk. The night's warmth felt good after the loud music and shouted conversations inside. Unlocking the driver's door, he reached for the pack in the center console. Screeching tires made him look up.

The black van screeched down the street at high speed, then turned fast into the Shipwreck's driveway. The tires squealed more as the driver completed the maneuver. The driver straightened and aimed the van at the building. Slayton's pulse raced. He was going to ram the wall—and did, crashing through the wall and windows to plow into patrons inside. The wall caved under the nose of the van, the glass shattering into pieces to rain on the pavement. The crash rang in Slayton's ears. Slayton left his smokes behind and started running.

The rear doors of the van swung open on wailing hinges, and the driver jumped out. He looked no worse for wear after the collision. When his feet hit the blacktop, he ran for the darkened building next door. He leaped over the hedge dividing the two properties and ran faster.

Slayton yelled, "Hey!" He wore his pressed tan uniform, his sinewy legs pumping as he ran for the driver. The driver looked back after leaping over the hedge, but in the low light, Slayton saw none of his facial features. Slayton ran halfway to the hedge and then—

The explosion began inside the van, a spark of orange fire filling the dirty windows. Then the orange fireball expanded, blasting the van apart as it also consumed the

Shipwreck. The ball of fire and thunder shook the ground and tossed Slayton off his feet. He hit the ground hard, but his yell of pain didn't overpower the noise of the blast as it lit the lot like day. Debris fell nearby, heavy chunks, sending jolts of panic through the SEAL commander as he tried to avoid getting pulverized. Slayton covered his face as he rolled and rolled until he reached a car. He crawled as far beneath the vehicle as space allowed. Another ground impact caught his attention, a soft, wet smack, and when he turned his head, he retched. Body parts. Stumps. Pieces of what used to be people. His friends were inside. His teammates. And innocent people, too. The fireball subsided and the fiery blaze took its place. The screams from within could only mimic the cries of the damned as they filled the night.

Commander Slayton watched and listened. There was no way for one man to stop it. He'd never felt so helpless in his life.

1

PRESENT DAY

The cartel soldiers loaded the hostages into the back by hand, as if loading lumber. The two males and two females had little choice but to comply. They were bound at the wrists and ankles. There was no way for them to fight or run. At least they weren't gagged.

But the lack of a gag was little consolation to Morgan Wright. She was the oldest of the four at twenty-three. They were too frightened to talk after the drug thugs explained what waited for them at the end of the ride. They were exhausted, starving, dirty. Morgan had no idea she could feel so filthy from head to toe. Their body odor was overpowering. All they'd done while in the tents was sweat. She'd been wearing the same clothes for three days. *Three days!* And each time they'd let her and Ana Edwards relieve themselves, in holes they had to dig, no less, the gunmen watched with leering eyes, obscene gestures, and snide remarks she understood all too well despite the language barrier.

The leader of the four gunmen, the one called Jorge, told them the plan. The US government didn't want them back. The president refused to let their families use a go-between for negotiations. So, they had no more need of them. They'd drop Morgan and Ana at a brothel. The men? Jorge only laughed. Morgan shook with a sudden chill and felt her heart palpitate. She tried to see the others, but there was no light. Only the sounds of nervous breathing. Body heat. Guttural Spanish from the two men guarding them. Morgan wondered if they were staring at her and Ana despite the lack of light.

They'd stared enough. Her pink tank was sweat-stained, dirty, and stretched. Instead of being an alluring sight for her boyfriend, her peek-a-boo breasts held the attention of men with only bad intentions. They hadn't paid as much attention to petite Ana. They liked Morgan's larger size better. The trip to Mexico was supposed to be a fun vacation after a tough semester. The plan at the end was for a celebration as Brody Lester asked Ana to marry him. Only Morgan knew—because Brody told her, of course. She suspected Cameron Hudson, *her* boyfriend, had an idea of what his university football teammate had in mind. Brody not acting like his usual jocular self made Ana wonder what was going on, too. Brody explained he was nervous about being in another country. Certainly understandable enough...

None of them had graduated college yet, but Brody told Morgan he couldn't wait. He wanted to get Ana "wifed up" ASAP. They'd work out the details later. They'd saved as much money as possible to afford a simple wedding. And now they were at the mercy of drug thugs who wanted to sell Ana and her to a brothel and murder Cam and Brody. She didn't blame the boys for not doing something heroic, not when the four thugs ambushed them with rifles. Football jocks or not, how do you fight four armed men with assault rifles when you have nothing to shoot back with? Especially the nasty-looking black rifles she always saw in movies. Cameron insisted on watching too many of those types of movies.

As the truck rumbled forward, tipping and rocking over the rough ground, Morgan attempted what she hoped had an effect. Something she hadn't done since she was small.

She shut her eyes and prayed.

* * *

JACK SLAYTON PEERED through his sniper scope and keyed a wireless com unit.

"Slayer to Alpha. They're moving the hostages, over."

He spoke just above a whisper. The sensitivity of the com unit meant he didn't have to raise his voice. The response, however, rang loud in his ear.

"Repeat, Slayer, over."

Slayton scoffed. "I said, *they're moving the hostages.* I am watching the bad guys drag the kids out of the tents and force them into the back of a large truck. If you don't get your asses in gear, there will not, repeat *not*, be any hostages to rescue. Copy?" He wanted to add, "*You idiot.*"

Slayton was a CIA "ghost" asset and part of the classified Z Section of the Special Activities Center. He was playing scout for a Ground Branch team tasked with getting the hostages home. They were American students who'd been hiking through Northern Mexico. A wrong turn brought them into cartel territory—or what the cartel *claimed* was their territory. The drug thugs grabbed the four students and made a big stink about American spies and invaders to the media with talking points straight from the al-Qaeda handbook. They wanted money or they promised to send the kids home in pieces—the males, anyway. The drug thugs said they'd sell the two women into the sex slave trade. The president didn't want to send the military. Instead, CIA Special Activities got the job. Ground Branch operators went into action.

Slayton's job was to provide cover for the rescue team. He hid within a cluster of rocks. He had fifty yards between him and the camp in which the drug crew put the students. They'd been there three days. Now the truck. And no sign of the rescue force. Slayton had the choice of watching from behind the scope of his MK14 rifle or taking action on his own.

"Read you clear, Slayer. We are three minutes out."

"They don't *have* three minutes," Slayton snapped. "Follow my GPS signal."

"Remain at post, Slayer, do you—"

Slayton did not copy. He yanked the com unit from his ear, switched off the power pack on his belt, and prepared to leave the rocks. Fifty yards. Yikes. But he kept in shape for such runs. It shouldn't be hard, he decided. *But who likes running?* He removed the scope from the rifle. He'd need iron sights for this. He didn't want to live with knowing he could have rescued the students, yet chose not to. He lived with enough guilt already from past situations and had no desire to add to the list. He wasn't equipped for a long fight. Rifle, pistol, no grenades. The drug gang carried HK rifles of the 5.56mm variety, great short-range shooters. He had to work fast.

One of the drug gunners shoved the last student into the covered truck. The engine rumbled to life.

Time to go, sport.

He left the rocks and broke into a run, aiming for a point ahead of the truck as it began to move. The dirt path wasn't smooth. None of the terrain was appropriate for vehicles. It was rougher on foot. At least the truck wasn't going to go fast. Two in the cabin, two in back, HK416s and perhaps other weapons, too.

Slayton hoped he wasn't about to get himself, or the students, killed.

2

Slayton ran hard, weaving around the rocks he could see, hoping he didn't trip on one he failed to notice. As he closed the distance with the big truck, he sought cover behind a patch of thorny brush. The support bipod under the MK14's handguard flipped down with a push of his left hand, and he lined up the iron sights. The truck's left front wheel was his first target. A snout extended from the rifle's muzzle—a suppressor. Slayton hoped they'd think a tire popped on a rock. He stroked the trigger. The rifle stock slammed against his shoulder. The tire popped, the truck stopped, and sank forward a little. A cloud of dust rose around the truck from the sudden braking, and the driver rolled down the window. He stuck his head out to look. A string of curses followed. Slayton settled the sights on the man's head. But he held his fire. He wanted the driver and passenger to investigate the blowout. If they had to jack up the truck and get a spare, they might unload the students first.

Wait. Not long...

The driver hopped out of the cab. He bent over to examine the tire. And started shouting. Well, dude knew bullet damage when he saw it. *There goes my plan!* Slayton switched to Plan B. He shot the driver in the back of the head to cut off his yelling. The driver's body slammed into the tire, his head bouncing off the rubber. Then his body flopped into the dirt.

The passenger hurried around the front of the truck. Slayton squeezed off another round. He felt the recoil once more and sent a boattail .308 slug through the man's brain. He never had a chance to see his dead comrade. The drug thug's body rustled loose rocks when he hit the ground. Slayton rose and started forward. A slow walk. He kept the rifle tight to his shoulder. If the last two didn't use the students as shields, he had a chance to nail them as they dropped out the back. But they didn't.

The two in the back began calling out to the driver and passenger. Slayton heard one name. *Jorge*. Which had he been? Slayton faced the side of the truck. The canvas cover over the back blocked his view inside. He stepped to the right. Kept his movement slow. He wanted a better view of the tailgate.

"Jorge?" one of the unseen gunmen called again. Finally, the gunner needed to see for himself. He swung one leg, then the other, out, resting the first on the back bumper. The rest of his body emerged, and—

Slayton shot him in the back.

The drug thug fell face first onto the edge of the tailgate. His head landed on the steel and made a *clang* echo through the night, then the rest of his body flopped on the ground. A woman inside screamed. It was a cry of panic. Slayton waited, breathing hard, anticipating the next gunman. He only had to wait two seconds. A slap cracked. A man yelled. The screaming stopped. Movement scraped the bed of the truck. The gunman started to come out, but stumbled. Somebody inside tripped him. He let out a surprised yell of his own as he flailed out the back. Crashing to the ground winded him. He was in no position to defend himself. Slayton fired twice. The gunman's body stayed on the ground.

Four enemy dead. *Good shooting.*

A male voice yelled, "Who's out there?"

Slayton approached the truck. "American soldier! We're here to take you home."

Slayton slung his rifle. He pressed a button on the GPS unit wrapped around his left wrist. The Ground Branch team would zero in on his signal. A flurry of excited voices filled the back of the truck. The four students scooted to the tailgate as fast as possible. Slayton lowered the gate and took out a knife. The sharp blade cut through the ropes binding their wrists and ankles. The two men were quiet, stoic. The women cried. The four jumped out and assaulted Slayton with hugs and thank yous. Slayton's attention wasn't on the students. He listened for further threats. Then the whipping sound of an approaching chopper filled the night.

Slayton led them away from the truck. Excitement ruled their emotions now. They couldn't stand still. Slayton ignored their rush of questions. He didn't answer the girl in the pink tank top when she asked for his name.

The big helicopter flew over. A spotlight lit the ground. One pass and scan, then the chopper set down. The rotor blast kicked up dirt and rocks and turned them into a storm of debris. Telling the students to shield their faces, Slayton led them into the chopper's cabin. Blue light lit the inside. It was low, but the faces of the other combat-ready operators stood out. The men helped the students into the cabin. One of the Ground Branch men glared at Slayton, who entered last. The crew chief slammed the side door closed. The chopper lifted off with a lurch, and they were airborne. The four students hugged as a group. Slayton heard them sobbing. He didn't know what they'd gone through, but it didn't matter. Trauma now united them. He hoped they'd be okay. He hoped their ordeal would fade into the ether with time. But he also knew they'd carry the experience with them the rest of their lives.

The Ground Branch team leader, still glaring, moved toward Slayton. "You disobeyed a direct order, Slayer. I'm saying so in my report."

"Spell my name right," Slayton snapped. The team leader stared at him through a tight frown. None of the Ground Branch team knew his name. He was *Slayer.* Nothing more.

The helicopter pilot steered north for home.

* * *

THE CHOPPER LANDED at an Air Force base in Texas. Medical personnel checked out the students and declared them fit, albeit dehydrated and in need of food and rest. But Slayton and the Ground Branch team didn't stay for the results. They went from the chopper to a waiting jet for the ride back to Virginia. The students would catch another flight home for the reunion with their families. The president would spin the rescue any way he wanted. Slayton wasn't interested in the words he chose.

Slayton knew he'd have to explain why he hadn't waited for the team, but a reprimand didn't bother him, either. The boss knew his methods by now. This hadn't been the first time he went into action alone, nor would it be the last. He had his arguments ready, but deep down he knew nothing he said would reveal the truth. He went in alone because one time he waited, and friends died. He swore then he'd never stand on the sidelines when he had the chance to do something. And his only answer to the inevitable, "What if you failed?" had only one reply: "But I didn't."

But next time, he knew, the odds might not be in his favor.

3

ALEXANDRA RUHL ADJUSTED THE MICROPHONE ON THE TABLE SO IT was closer. She didn't think the committee could hear her.

The men and women seated on the raised crescent dais weren't trying to intimidate her, but she still sensed a challenge in their eyes. *Prove yourself.* Perhaps, Alexandra decided, she only saw in them what she thought about herself. She didn't have to prove anything to them. But to herself? She still had a *lot* to prove.

She addressed the annual EU Convention on World Hunger. Her testimony concerned the effort of her charity to feed the starving people of the world. She and her staff brought visual material, pictures and videos, to fill in any gaps in her verbal descriptions. Since she was working under funding from the EU, they wanted a full update. Her facts, figures, and pictures of smiling faces filled a jumbo screen to the left of the dais.

"Our plan to deliver grain, wheat, and set up clean water filtration systems in villages exceeded our expectations," she told them. Her German accent wasn't as thick as it had once been, but her roots remained unmistakable. "When we started, nine out of ten villages lacked a clean water source. Our results for the year brought that number down to seven out of ten, and our goal this year is to close the gap further. The slides on the screen now show our crews installing filtration systems. Here is a crew teaching village leaders how to maintain them. We had to add regular checkup visits this year because too many forgot our instructions. They'd do the procedures wrong or not at all. Our return visits have kept water filtration running at one hundred percent."

The slide changed to show a photo collage of farms in various stages of growth. Empty ditches to full harvests.

"We did the same with our farming program," Alexandra continued, "with regular return visits. Now villages can grow their own grain, corn, and vegetables. This means fewer starving people waiting for a truck to unload what they need to survive."

The slide changed to a video montage. Cranes loaded large white bags showing the blue logo of Alexandra's organization onto cargo ships. A crew on an airplane shoved parachute-rigged pallets off an open ramp.

"We operate in crisis mode," she said. "It's an organized crisis, though. It gives us a sense of urgency every day. We rely on a global network for shipping, and we've reduced our losses and waste to half of what we suffered last year. We intend to decrease losses further this year with greater oversight of our network. To do so, we've hired more people."

The panel may not have been intimidating on purpose. But two dozen pairs of eyes staring at her made Alexandra's stomach flutter with nervous tension. This was a friendly crowd, she reminded herself. No need to panic.

They have to be pleased with this, she thought, taking a pause to sip from a glass of warm water. The hearing room was small, circular, with wood-paneled walls.

"Now," she resumed, "instead of putting you all to sleep with more facts and figures, why don't we take a moment to answer questions."

She smiled her killer smile, her teeth shining white, straight, perfect.

Alexandra Ruhl showed up dressed to kill, too. Blue blazer, skirt with the hem above the knee, white V-neck blouse. To make sure she didn't flash the panel, a camisole under the blouse took up the space the V-neck otherwise revealed. Her long brown hair fell down her shoulders and back. Nobody was close enough to see her favorite feature—the rich brown eyes that took in every detail. She was sunshine and glamour. She didn't care who knew it, or saw it, or what they thought about it.

The panel offered routine questions. Alexandra answered each in detail and even showed other portions of her visual data to fill any gaps. When she resumed, she talked about money. She emphasized how much the organization needed to reach the following year's goals. The panel listened with rapt attention. Putty in her hand, she hoped. Unless they told her no. She didn't think they would. Her organization existed as a feather in the cap of the EU. Something to brag about to the United Nations. By the time the hearing ended two hours later, Alexandra Ruhl had the promise of a funding increase. She didn't hold back her smile.

* * *

ALEXANDRA RUHL SETTLED into the back of her limousine with a satisfied sigh. Her driver merged into traffic. The hearing was over and a success. Now she had more pressing matters to attend to. She allowed herself a moment, though. A moment to sit and reflect and remember the man who wasn't alive to see her success. Her husband. He would have been proud of her. Another smile, tinged with sadness. Before the melancholy took over, she reached for the telephone hanging near the door. The number she dialed from memory.

A man answered the phone.

"Yes?"

"It's me," she said.

"Did we get the money?"

"All of it. We keep up the feeding program, and we'll funnel the extra into our other plans."

"Speaking of..." the man said.

"Are you set for tonight?"

"We're ready. Once it's finished, we'll dump Karina's body where the CIA can find her."

"They better get the message."

"They will," the man said.

"I'll watch for the results."

Alexandra ended the call and leaned back. The ride continued, the outside noise muffled, the interior quiet, Alexandra staring out but not seeing anything. Her mind was elsewhere, thinking about the discovery of a traitor within her ranks. How much damage the traitor might have done. She'd have answers shortly.

Soon, her chauffeur would drop her at the airport where

a private jet waited to take her home. The staff who'd accompanied her to the hearing were taking regular flights. Being the boss had many perks. Private travel was one of them.

Alexandra Ruhl wasn't the charity angel the media and public believed. The charity was only a cover. She was the leader of the New Red Army Faction, and the charity partially funded her war machine. Both were the brainchild of her late husband, who dreamed of seeing a global communist revolution fueled by the passions of young people willing to put their lives on the line. Half of Europe was already primed and ready for such a change, but the holdouts needed a push. The New Red Army Faction was there to provide the necessary push even if it meant setting the West on fire. She had big plans and big ideas and the means with which to make them happen. When the time came to claim victory over the past, a past full of bloodshed and oppression, she'd show the world what real leadership looked like.

4

NUMBER SIX SWUNG HIS BAT AS THE PITCHER LAUNCHED THE BALL. *Crack*. The ball flew to the outfield at light speed, and three kids with their mitts ready converged to grab the ball. Number Six raced to first base. He reached the plate before the outfielders caught the ball. Parents representing both of the little league teams cheered the kids on.

Jack Slayton watched from far away, using a tree for cover. He smiled as he watched Number Six run. The boy was growing up fast. He looked healthy. Another batter stepped up to the plate. More cheering from eager parents.

"I thought I'd find you here."

Slayton turned. His smile turned to a frown.

The new arrival said, "I've been calling but you aren't answering your phone."

Slayton turned back to the game. "It's my day off." He tried to watch the game, but the activity wasn't registering now.

"Something has come up, and I need you," the other man said.

Slayton cursed.

"Wait, is this—"

"Yes, Nate, that's Hank Downing's kid, and his widow on the top bleacher, who doesn't want me coming near her son in case I convince him to do the same thing that got his father killed. Keep your voice down."

"I give the orders, Jack. Your tone is unprofessional."

Slayton grumbled something.

"I didn't hear you."

"I said, I liked my old boss better."

Slayton's old boss was Dylan Sharp, and the pair were close friends. But Sharp was gone. He left the CIA for the private sector after the unfortunate incidents of a few months prior. Now Nathan Mason ran Z Section. The secret unit was a Special Access Program and covered a variety of diverse tasks, but all shared a common trait: operations beyond top secret. Z Section managed what other clandestine units couldn't handle.

Nobody liked Mason. He was an overbearing jerk at best. There was only one person in the office Slayton and his fellow shooters liked. She was Slayton's girlfriend, Reema Ashraf. She "handled" most of them while in the field. The relationship between Jack and Reema wasn't something Nathan Mason approved of, but there was also nothing he could do about it.

"What do you want me to do?" Slayton said. He turned back to Mason with folded arms. The park's car lot was only ten yards behind them. They were far from prying eyes.

"I'd prefer we talk in my car," Mason said.

"Lead the way."

Mason was older, late sixties, and should have retired

years ago. For some reason, the Agency let him keep working. White-haired, bald on top, and an imposing six-footer, Mason had extensive field experience which he now brought to his role as leader of Z Section. He achieved results and protected his people. But he was also a demanding, abrasive, insufferable ass.

The two men convened in Mason's white town car, a relic from the '90s. Mason refused to buy a new car. And it was more than stubbornness or lack of funds. He didn't like how the heavy tech in new vehicles made them vulnerable to electronic attack. "Hack" a car, force the driver into a tree at high speed—it wasn't outside the realm of possibility. It was a terrific assassination ploy, and one Mason wanted to avoid.

Tinted side windows blocked out most of the light outside. Slayton had to admit the soft seats felt good to sit in. Mason, behind the wheel, turned the ignition key to crack the windows.

"All right," Mason said. "I need you in Berlin. *Tonight.*"

"We have people in Berlin. Why me?"

"Because *Lonesome Dove* is coming in, and you need to be there."

Slayton was too stunned to reply right away.

Lonesome Dove. The code name given to Karina Radler, a German woman involved in a terrorist group called the New Red Army Faction. Slayton recruited her as an agent to discover the whereabouts of one of her comrades, a man named Andreas Ritter, the one responsible for the bombing of the Shipwreck Bar so many years before. The man responsible for killing a score of innocent civilians and many of his SEAL teammates. Karina provided good intelligence, but Ritter's location remained a mystery. He vanished after the Shipwreck bombing. The CIA's hunt for the terrorist was cataloged, appropriately enough, as Operation Iron Ghost, and its lack of success frustrated many at CIA HQ. If Karina was coming in from the cold, maybe she finally had the answers they were looking for.

"Did she find Ritter?" Slayton asked.

"Better. She found the top dog. This is a big one, Jack. Extends from Germany well into European industry, perhaps EU leadership itself. She contacted us while you were in Mexico. We only got the pick-up information two hours ago. You'd have known sooner if you answered your phone."

"It's my *day off*, Nate. Do you answer your phone when not working?"

"I'm always working."

Slayton scoffed.

"Go home and pack. You leave in four hours. Reema will provide your flight details."

"Okay." Slayton opened the door and started to get out.

"Good luck, Jack. I know you've worked hard on this."

"Thanks." Slayton left the car and closed the door. He heard another crack and cheers from the baseball diamond. He'd have liked to watch the rest of the game. But duty called. Karina needed help, and Slayton couldn't refuse if he tried.

* * *

Slayton paused his packing when someone knocked on the door.

He left the bedroom, grabbing a Colt Viper revolver from the nightstand. He wasn't expecting company.

He moved quickly down the hall, left into the entryway, and a glance through the peephole...

Slayton grinned at the sight opposite. Reema stood in the hall. He wondered why she wore an overcoat buttoned to her neck. He wondered why she hadn't used her key.

He tucked the revolver in the waistband of his jeans and opened the door.

"Is it cold out?"

"Let me in." She laughed.

"You have a key, hon."

"Let me *in*," she said. "You're ruining my seduction technique."

"Oh."

He stepped back. She entered. They shared the two-bedroom condo in McLean, not far from CIA HQ. Neither were the best housekeepers, and clutter was always within sight. He closed the door. She eyed him up and down and settled on where he'd stuck the Colt.

"Nice bulge in your pants," she said.

"The Colt variety." He took out the gun and told her to follow him to the bedroom.

Reema Ashraf carried the weight of her world in every graceful step—tall and trim, her olive skin glowing, showing off her European Iraqi roots. Waves of dark hair framed her face and tumbled freely down her back. Her eyes, deep pools of brown etched by past loss and peril, held a quiet storm, yet they flickered with a spark of girlish innocence and tender vulnerability. Her body, honed by survival's demands into a lithe, attention-commanding form, turned heads without invitation—curves subtle yet insistent. Despite her honed skills and fighting experience shaped by the necessity of survival, she wasn't a field operative. Her true strength lay in analyzing data, uncovering insights others missed.

A former Iraqi intelligence officer, Reema defected to the US and joined the CIA. Her deep understanding of the Middle East and counterterrorism made her an invaluable asset.

They had been a couple for several years, with an unfortunate three-year gap when she went undercover and disappeared. Missing in action, presumed killed. But she was back, in his arms, alive and well, but their reunion met its share of resistance. The frowns from Mason had nothing to do with their challenges. Reconnecting after such a long gap, and the trauma Reema experienced during their time apart, meant they couldn't pick up where they left off no matter how much they wanted to. Instead, they had to work through the trauma.

"I brought your flight stuff, and thought I'd give you a ride to the airport," she said.

"I'll take it," he said. Slayton resumed packing. He told her to talk as he worked. She set her purse on the dresser, but didn't remove the overcoat.

"Don't worry about Mexico," she said.

Slayton loaded a shirt, jeans, and underwear into his suitcase. "I'm not."

"I mean, the Deputy Director finished his review. There will be no reprimand. He's more concerned with what delayed the rescue team."

"A circle jerk, probably."

Slayton added a shaving kit and zipped the case closed. He lifted it off the bed and set it on the floor.

"Now," he said, "what's with the coat?"

Reema undid the buttons down the front, opened the

coat, revealing her blouse and skirt, dark stockings and black heels. She began unbuttoning her blouse, the fabric slipping from her shoulders to reveal the secrets underneath.

"We don't have time, hon," he said.

"Excuse me? Eyes up here, Mr. Slayton."

He laughed.

"We can make the time." She shed the rest of her clothes and let them fall on the floor. The stockings landed on the pile last.

"Won't take long," she said.

"Well—"

She stepped close to him. Her naked body radiated heat. She put her arms around his neck and pressed close.

"Now I feel a different bulge," she said, grinning.

"Honey—"

"Fifteen minutes."

"I'll need a shower after," he said. "It'll take more than fifteen minutes, and I'll miss my flight."

"I'll help you," she said.

The room grew warmer. Her eyes held his, vulnerable yet bold.

Their three-year gap had stretched between them like an unbridgeable chasm. They'd had to rediscover each other. Slayton had to adjust to how her experience changed her. Her laugh wasn't the same. Some of her carefree attitude was gone, replaced by cautious behavior, second glances, careful steps. She had bouts of melancholy, moments when she stared into space, reliving horrors she only spoke of in whispers. She had new scars. But her hand still fit perfectly in his. It hadn't been easy—conversations late into the night, tentative touches rebuilding a broken bond—but the effort had forged a connection stronger than before, much deeper than before, like roots intertwining after a storm.

A few minutes wouldn't hurt, he decided. She helped him undress, and they moved to the bed and had a silent conversation of skin on skin, breaths mingling in the hush of the room. Every caress was a reaffirmation, every sigh a promise rediscovered, their intimacy a bridge over the years lost.

When it ended, Reema, beneath him, held Slayton tight, her arms wrapped around him as if to anchor him to the moment. "Promise you won't leave me," she whispered, her voice trembling.

He nibbled on her right earlobe. She moaned softly. "I won't."

Slayton didn't miss his flight.

5

Karina Radler's arms were already numb, stretched out on either side, immobile. As she regained consciousness, she felt the tight rubber straps bite into her wrists and ankles. The straps were wrapped around the legs of the table on which she lay. She still had her clothes on. Her head hurt from where somebody had hit her prior to leaving her apartment.

Karina figured she wasn't going to make her pick-up with Slayton after all.

She tried to breathe regularly and willed herself to stay calm.

Only a bulb dangling from the ceiling lit the room. Bare concrete walls and floor. The surrounding shadows may have covered exits, but she had no way to tell. This place was unfamiliar. Not the same spot they'd interrogated traitors and captives in the past. *Traitor. Captive.* The irony did not escape her. She tried to move, but no dice. The straps held firm. She had nothing to do but wait.

Slow footsteps. Closer. Louder. Karina's pulse quickened.

A man named Markus Frenz stepped into the light. The eyes in his ugly face gazed on her with contempt. They had been friends and comrades-in-arms for years. Now, he was going to kill her. And she had no idea how the organization discovered her subterfuge.

"Hello, Karina."

She met his eyes but said nothing. She repeated a mantra in her head. A simple one. Stay calm.

"It's only us down here," Frenz said. "My men are upstairs with orders not to come down no matter how much you scream."

Stay calm. Stay calm. Stay calm.

Her pulse thundered in her skull.

"You've given us all a shock, Karina. Some don't believe it's true. But it is true, isn't it?"

Karina pressed her lips together.

"You won't deny it?" He moved his left hand to his hip. He wore a pistol on the right side, but his left hand hovered over the hilt of a combat knife. Frenz pulled the knife from the scabbard. The stainless-steel blade shone in the light. He held it casually, as if about to slice a steak on the bias. Karina's stoic expression changed a little. Fright entered her eyes.

Staycalmstaycalmstaycalm...

"We're going to have a talk, Karina." He placed the side of the blade against her cheek. It was cold. She shivered. He moved it from her cheek to her chin, letting the razor edge rub against her pale skin. She didn't feel it cut, but her body trembled in response anyway.

He rubbed the blade along her other cheek.

"You're very pretty, Karina. I've always admired your looks. Do you remember what you said when I suggested we should date? You didn't think soldiers should be romantic with each other. But that didn't stop you from later making *Hans* your lover. Now I have two reasons to hate you."

The razor edge crossed her chin again. He moved to her right cheek for another pass and Karina stiffened.

Stay. Calm. Stay...

The blade drifted to her button-down flannel shirt. She looked like a buxom farm girl with the shirt and jeans. She had wanted to be comfortable when she met Slayton.

Markus Frenz didn't bother with the buttons. He grabbed the fabric and used the blade to slice down the front. The tearing sounded almost like a shriek from a crow as the first whimper finally escaped Karina's lips.

Frenz grinned at her. "You *can* make noises!"

Karina pressed her lips together. Droplets of sweat formed on her forehead and trickled down the side of her face.

Frenz sliced away more of her clothing. Her chest heaved up and down as she tried to calm herself once more, but it was a lost cause. Frenz reached her belt and tugged the rest of her shirt free, slashed with the knife, and flung the fabric open on either side, as if he'd gutted a fish. She lay on the table bound and trembling, her stomach quivering, chest heaving, a sheen of sweat on her white skin.

She shut her eyes tight.

The mantra was useless now. Karina knew she'd die in this room, on the table. Nobody was coming to save her.

* * *

Markus Frenz said, "Tell me what you gave the Americans." He leaned close to her. He wanted to smell her fear. "How much damage have you done?"

Karina's mouth twisted, and she spat in his face. He recoiled, his left hand swinging, striking her in return. Karina's head jerked to one side, the sound of the slap like a gunshot in the quiet room. She made no other sound. He wiped his face, then gripped the knife harder and sliced open her bra, flinging the cups to either side. Karina whimpered a little, but bit her bottom lip to cut off further noise.

"I want to know what you told them. I want to know why you betrayed us. What was the reason, Karina?"

She finally raised her voice in reply.

"Go to hell!"

"You gave as much to the cause as the rest of us. Why throw it away?"

Karina was breathing fast, trying to shift her body, but finding no freedom of movement.

"Tell me what I want to know!"

"No!"

Frenz froze, staring at her, but not with lust. Instead, he stared with revulsion.

He knew the answer to part of the question.

"I know why," he said. "Because of Hans. Of course! We dealt with him as a suspected traitor, and *then* you plotted your treachery in revenge. It makes sense now, Karina."

"So get this *over* with!"

"But we aren't finished." He laughed. "Tell me what you gave the Americans. I know the why. Now tell me the what."

"No!"

Frenz's arm moved in a flash. He pulled out the knife

and slammed the tip of the blade into the table. The point landed less than half an inch from Karina's right leg. She squeaked out of fear, then pressed her lips together. She watched the knife.

"Tell me."

He pulled the blade from the table.

"No!"

Slam! Karina screamed. The blade was closer this time.

"You're going to kill me anyway! What do I care?"

He had to work the knife out this time, shifting it back and forth to pull the blade from the wooden table. The two cuts were like scars on the tabletop. Karina tried to shift once more but failed to create more space between her and the table's edge.

"You're right," Frenz said.

Alexandra Ruhl wasn't going to like hearing Frenz learned nothing. It was Karina's last thought, her last strike back against those who killed Hans for no reason. They'd be left to wonder...

Frenz swung the knife down a final time.

6

KARINA WAS LATE.

Slayton waited in the doorway of a closed shop. The shopping center faced an empty street, and he was alone with the crickets and streetlamps. He arrived earlier in the afternoon and reported to the embassy. The local CIA staff informed him of the pick-up location and time, and Slayton left on schedule. An hour had passed since Karina was supposed to arrive. Slayton had a car parked in front of the shop, less than ten feet to his right. He waited in the doorway so he could run and shoot should the need arise. In the doorway, he had a solid backstop, and a full view of the area in front of him.

He carried his CZ P-10C autoloader. The 9mm pistol rode in a shoulder holster under his right armpit. The pistol wasn't standard issue, but instead his personal weapon, one he'd counted on during many missions and had yet to let him down.

Slayton's instinct was to call his contact at the embassy and report Karina's failure to show. An informant over an hour late wasn't coming, and he had no way to reach her quickly. Their past interaction had only been via dead drop or coded email. Slayton had worked hard to keep her activity concealed, but the safeguards had failed, somehow. Still, he waited. Just in case. He owed her the extra time.

A car drove by now and then, but at this hour, well after 0300, any motorists on the road had places to go. The streetlamps and lot lights burned with a muted buzz. It was the only sound other than his breathing.

When he first recruited Karina, he doubted she was trustworthy.

She said her colleagues executed her lover, who they'd suspected of selling the New Red Army Faction's weapons to other terror cells, after a mock trial. She feared they'd kill her too, but she was a cell leader. They needed her. Instead, her comrades tried to justify the execution, and she went along. Betraying the terror group was her way of getting even. Despite his doubts, Slayton put her to work. And, to his surprise, she'd provided crucial intelligence about the cell structure, sources of weapons and money, and other valuable pieces, but never the piece Slayton wanted. She'd never determined the location of Andreas Ritter.

Had Karina somehow tipped her hand? Had her people been watching for such a development? Or was he letting his mind play tricks on him, and she was safe, on her way, but taking precautions? Slayton checked his watch. 0355. She was now almost two hours late.

* * *

THE VAN BUMPED over the rough road. Karina Radler let out a choked cry through the gag over her mouth. She was on the floor in the back, two men up front, two more—including Frenz—inches from where she lay.

The van was dark, only flashes from streetlights broke through the windows. The flashes revealed Frenz's face. He stared at her. She avoided his gaze. His humiliation of her was nothing compared to failing to avenge Hans. She'd failed to get the CIA the most important piece of information she'd ever give them.

Frenz hadn't killed her at the torture house. His last slam of the knife into the table had been between her thighs. He'd made it clear where he wanted to cut her and leave her to bleed out, but he still needed her to send a message to the CIA. And he hadn't wanted to drive with her dead body leaking and stinking up the van.

It added up to one thing, Karina knew. As long as she remained alive, she had a chance. With her hands and ankles still tied, she wasn't sure what to do should she discover the opportunity to escape. They were going to the pick-up spot where Slayton waited. Maybe he'd provide the chance she needed.

The van slowed.

"We're here," the driver announced. He turned the wheel to the right.

Frenz drew his gun and screwed on a suppressor.

"Goodbye, Karina."

She tried to scream as he pressed the snout to her forehead.

Darkness enveloped her.

* * *

Slayton shifted and dropped into a crouch when the van entered the parking lot. It approached from the left, moving parallel to the storefronts. He drew the P-10C and his pulse quickened. The van came abreast of the shop, and the side door flew open. Two men dressed in black, framed themselves in the doorway. They opened fire with stubby submachine guns. The roar of the firepower echoed through the night.

Slayton rolled forward, across the concrete walkway, off the curb with a thud, and out onto the parking lot blacktop. The bullets sizzled overhead, shattering glass, whining off painted brick. The van passed. A body fell out and tumbled onto the blacktop. The van sped off with a screech and turned back onto the street.

Slayton rose, keeping the van in the sights of his pistol, but holding his fire. Light shone on the body. He turned his attention to the crumpled form. Blue jeans, flannel shirt, long blonde—

No!

Slayton ran to Karina's body and turned her face into the light. Blood soaked her hair, her forehead cored by a bullet. The exit wound in back was large. The pool of blood and brain matter beneath her blended with the blacktop. He stood and put away his gun. Nothing to do now but get away before the Berlin police arrived. He went to his car. With a cold, stoic expression, Slayton dropped behind the wheel and started the engine.

There was nothing he could do for her. The enemy reached her first. All he could do was, somehow, avenge her. He drove away with one last glance at Karina's body in the rearview mirror. His hands tightened on the wheel.

Someone was going to pay.

* * *

Slayton drove to the embassy at Pariser Platz 2. The Marine guards checked his ID and authorization and let him through the gate.

He signed in with the desk security officer, then used a special key card to access a basement-level office via elevator. A short hallway led to a door marked "restricted," but the key card allowed entry.

He stepped through into the CIA Berlin command center. A room full of desks with computer workstations. Staffers occupied a few of the desks but most remained empty. The overnight supervisor approached. His name was Hector. Long graying beard, bald dome, stocky build. Slayton liked him for his dark sense of humor, but the look on his face indicated there'd be no jokes tonight.

"You're alone."

Slayton had to fight to say, "Nice observation," but the ambush and murder of Karina wasn't Hector's fault. There was no need to take it out on him.

"It all went to hell," Slayton said. "We lost our asset. I need a secure room."

"Down the hall, first on the left."

Slayton proceeded where indicated. He shut the door to the small room with white walls, thin blue carpets, table, and all-in-one desktop. He fired up the computer and adjusted the camera atop the PC. After logging in, he initiated a video call with home base. Reema Ashraf's face filled the box on the screen. She wore regular business clothes as opposed to his street clothes. But he had to open with a zinger despite his mood.

"Where's the overcoat?"

"Back in the closet," she said. "The Old Buzzard made me wait for when you called. It's after six here. I should be home."

"He needs his beauty sleep more than you," Slayton said. *As if it would do any good.* He didn't verbalize the thought. He updated Reema on the situation and Reema expressed her sympathies.

She added, "The boss won't be happy. We'll have to smooth things over with the Germans because there wasn't supposed to be any shooting."

"Tell the Old Buzzard and the krauts the shooting wasn't my idea."

"What do you want to do now?"

"I'm thinking Karina may have left a clue behind, a dead man's switch."

"You mean a dead woman switch?"

"You know what I mean, Reema."

"You want me to go through her file?"

"And what she's already told us. There may be a lead somewhere. And I could be talking out of my ass, too. I'm not getting back on a plane for home until I try."

"I'll look on this end. Good luck and be careful."

"I will."

She smiled. "I miss you."

"I miss you too, hon."

"I love you."

He laughed. He wondered if the Old Buzzard realized the call would end this way. He didn't like them having a relationship. He'd hate them talking mushy over a secure video link.

Slayton smiled shyly. "Same, babe."

There were some things even *he* didn't want to say over a vid call.

She ended the connection and the screen returned to the standard desktop view.

Slayton remained in the chair for a moment. Then, with a sigh, he began accessing the Lonesome Dove case file and searched for a literal needle in a haystack. He read past reports and choked on coffee till he was bleary-eyed. But after three hours, he had half a page of written notes and an idea. Problem was, the other side likely had the same idea, and didn't need three hours to find it.

7

Nathan Mason entered his office the next morning and hung up his coat. His glass-fronted office looked out on a busy bullpen. The analysts and mission controllers assigned to Z Section were always busy. Chatter filled the room. Nobody sat still for long, bouncing out of their chairs to handle various matters like gophers on a golf course. On the opposite side, mission specialists monitored real-time operator activity.

He read Reema's update on Berlin and cursed. His mood turned sour fast. He had to deal with the situation before Slayton found himself in more trouble. Hopefully, he was laying low till further notice. Mason picked up the phone and dialed his counterpart in Berlin.

He reached the office of Rolf Gerheardt and asked the secretary to put him through. Gerheardt was the supervisor for the counterterror unit of the Bundeskriminalamt, or BKA, Germany's equivalent to the US FBI.

"Gerheardt speaking," the German answered.

"Rolf. Nate Mason."

"I expected to hear from you much sooner."

"We're dealing with the blowback," Mason said. "My apologies. We planned on a simple pick-up."

"And now I have a dead terrorist in the morgue and a lot of questions. Your man has not made himself available to answer any."

"My man is waiting for orders," Mason said. "You'll have your chance to talk to him. I'm going to ask for your indulgence for a short time, Rolf. We need to find out how this happened and decide where we go next."

"You better hope the Faction doesn't retaliate. With a bomb. Or worse."

"They're doing damage control now," Mason said. "They will be more concerned with what our asset leaked."

"I don't share your optimism."

"Then let me suggest we pool our resources. I'll have our man get in touch right away."

"If the Faction goes active, lives are at stake. I need to speak with my superiors first. They may edge you out, Nathan."

"You'd be within your rights, of course. But we've done good work together, and you know as much as you do about the Faction because of our asset."

"I'll make the case, but no promises."

"I appreciate it, Rolf."

Mason hung up, lifted the receiver again, and dialed Slayton's cell.

* * *

Markus Frenz watched his men work.

He and four others were at Karina's apartment, and

they tore the place apart. They wanted to find any written record of what she'd provided to the CIA. His crew littered the floor with tossed items. The furniture lay in shreds where they'd looked for anything she may have hidden. So far, they'd discovered nothing. She covered her tracks well.

Frenz wandered, not making any comments as his men worked. He examined a wall of hanging photographs. It was easy to hide things in picture frames, he decided. He stopped when he found a picture of Karina and another woman who was a little taller than her. Both women wore bikinis and posed on the deck of a big boat. Karina filled out her pink bikini well, and her *sister* matched her attributes.

Karina's sister. Iva.

Frenz told his men to wrap up. The search was over. The sister was the lead they needed. He was certain.

* * *

SLAYTON SAT in the hotel restaurant eating a very late breakfast of bacon, eggs, hash browns, and toast. His watch showed it was after noon.

His cell rang. He looked at the screen. *Mason.*

Time for a lecture.

"Yes, boss."

"Where are you?"

"Eating breakfast very late."

"More like wasting your time. The Germans are threatening to cut us out of this if we don't get it sorted."

"I was up all night, Nate."

"Doing what?"

Slayton explained his review and what he found. "Her

sister, Iva. Karina may have passed something to her in case anything happened."

"Well, *great* job not going to her right away. You should have gotten her out of bed."

"Hey, I gotta sleep and eat, Nate."

"Eat and sleep and shit on your own time. The clock is ticking, and we're behind. The Germans are afraid of retaliation."

"I can't control the Germans, Nate."

"I want you to go see Rolf Gerheardt as soon as you can."

"Will do."

"And I want to know how they discovered Karina and knew about the meet."

"Bad things happen, Nate. You can do everything right and still get killed."

"Not good enough for me," Mason said. "Find out."

"Okay."

"Now. Tell me about the sister."

Slayton took a deep breath. He wanted the call over with. But the boss always needed more details.

"Her name is Iva, and they used to be close. Parents are dead, so she's the only family Karina had. Karina's politics caused a rift, but the sister is worth talking to."

"Then hit the road. We need to know. It may be a long shot, though. Our best bet may be a full assault against the Faction, but that's Gerheardt's call, not mine."

And it drives you nuts, doesn't it? Slayton grinned at the unspoken thought. He promised to do what he could and to see Gerheardt. Mason hung up without a goodbye. Slayton picked at his food. He wasn't hungry any longer. He waved the waiter over and asked for his check.

* * *

Markus Frenz grew tired of waiting, but Alexandra Ruhl lived by her own schedule.

He paced the top-floor office in downtown Berlin. He didn't often visit the offices of her charity organization, but the urgency demanded an exception. He appreciated how hard she worked on the legitimate side. The charity provided cover for the not-so-legit activities of the New Red Army Faction.

The office was huge, with her desk by the window, a sitting area, and a small conference table. He could have sat while waiting. But he was too keyed up. He needed action. He hoped Alexandra agreed with his idea of picking up Karina's sister. Maybe he could have fun with her, too. He'd enjoy hearing her scream when she saw his knife.

The office door swung open, and Alexandra Ruhl entered with purpose. She looked good in her suit. The pencil skirt hugged her flaring hips, alluring black stockings encased her legs. She wasn't happy, and her fiery eyes let him know without question. She snapped at him to sit as she took the big chair behind her desk.

"Tell me you have an idea."

Frenz explained about Iva Radler.

"Did our surveillance show Karina talking to her sister at all? I thought they were estranged."

Frenz admitted they had no record of Karina interacting with her sister.

"So why do you think the sister has any idea what Karina wanted to tell the Americans?"

"We don't have a lot of options, Alexandra."

"No, we don't. The apartment revealed nothing?"

Frenz shook his head. "Only the sister."

"She wanted to tell them about *me*, Markus. It's the only thing that makes sense."

"And Ritter."

"What?"

"They want you to lead them to Andreas."

"Yes. Yes, that makes even *more* sense. Get the sister. Do *not* harm her right away."

Frenz agreed. Alexandra dismissed him and didn't show him to the door.

8

Alexandra remained seated after Frenz departed. She turned her chair to look out at the Berlin skyline.

Her late husband dreamed of the New Red Army Faction, but it was she who nursed the dream to fulfillment. The capitalists of the world were the enemy, and she wanted to take the war to their doorstep. It amused her to have so many big money donors from the wealthy class flocking to her charity, begging to write bigger checks every year. They had no idea they were financing their own destruction while using the money to bury the guilt over what their greed caused. The New Red Army Faction would bring power to the people oppressed by the wealthy elite. She relished the idea of putting her boots on their necks. The necks of those who used greed to harm too many.

The New Faction wasn't a product of hasty planning, however. Alexandra studied the original Red Army Faction, its leaders, objectives, actions, and results. She wanted to amplify their success while avoiding their mistakes.

Also known as the Baader-Meinhof Group, the original

Red Army Faction was most active in the 1970s, but existed as late as 1998 before the group disbanded. By then, its original leaders were dead or in prison. The leaders who followed the founders never made as big an impact, but they'd had a long reach. Founders Andreas Baader, Ulrike Meinhof, and Gudrun Ensslin wanted to destroy capitalism and imperialism and replace it with solid Marxist-Leninist ideology. West Germany wasn't their only target. They included the United States on their hit lists, too.

Training for the original Red Army Faction took place in Jordan alongside Palestinian fighters. Money came from the Soviet Union and East Germany. They were puppets in the Cold War, sent into action by leaders who claimed ignorance of the matter while trying to talk peace with the imperial West. More of their funding came through bank robberies, and it was there that Alexandra drew a line.

She didn't want the police hunting her people over a few thousand bucks, and the Soviets were history. There'd be no funding from another country this time. No, the way to fund the New Faction was to take advantage of the people they wanted to kill. Take their money first. Make them happy about writing big checks. So, a charity.

Her late husband's dream became her dream, too. Part of her wished he was alive to see it, but she was having too much fun to share.

* * *

Iva Radler tried to hide her distaste as her colleague Ernst slipped into the elevator. The doors rumbled shut. She felt his leering eyes on her as the elevator car began to descend.

"Busy day, Iva?"

"Yes." His too-strong cologne almost made her retch. His suit looked rumpled after a long day at the office. He was taller than her and made her feel small—which was saying something, as her height topped out at nearly six feet.

"I bet you want to do something to relax," he said.

"Nothing with you, Ernst."

He laughed. "Come on. Have a drink with me."

"And we'll see how it goes?"

"You read my mind."

"No, Ernst. I'm not saying it again."

The elevator touched down in the lobby. The doors opened, and she started out. Ernst and his long strides didn't have to work hard to keep up. Plus, with her skirt, stockings, and heels, it was tough to move as fast as she wanted. If she'd been in jeans or her jogging outfit, she'd have outrun the son of a bitch.

"Iva, please, you misunderstand me."

"It's pretty obvious, Ernst."

Her heels tapped on the tiled floor, giving off an echo in the mostly glass lobby. Steel beams made perfect squares of the window glass. The hard-working AC kept it from becoming a giant greenhouse.

He grabbed her arm. She jerked away and faced him head-on.

"Ernst, stop it!" It was good to put on a show in front of witnesses and cameras. Especially the cameras. "If you keep this up, I'm claiming harassment. Stop it right now."

"Iva—" Ernst glanced over her shoulder. She turned to see what had closed his big mouth. Two men in light-colored suits stood there. One held a police badge.

"Miss Radler?"

Confusion clouded her face, then alarm. A chill raced over her, and the AC wasn't to blame.

Her sister.

Her voice shook. "Yes."

"You need to come with us, please."

"What for?"

"There's been an accident."

"Tell me now."

Ernst stepped between her and the cops. "Is your ID for real? The seal is wrong."

The man who did the talking moved in a flash. His right hand pushed back the flap of his coat—to grab a stun gun? Iva had seen them on television and wished she could afford one and German law allowed her to carry. It would come in handy when dealing with Ernst! But then the cop fired at Ernst, the wired prongs embedding into his stomach through his shirt. The crackle of electricity was louder than she expected, and she jumped back, startled.

As Ernst screamed and collapsed, the second cop made his move. He grabbed for Iva. This time she screamed as he twisted her around so her back was against him. But her purse blocked the "cop" from getting cuffs on her. She used the pause to raise one heeled foot and bring it down *hard* on his left shoe.

The man yelled. His grip slackened. Iva broke free. She ran across the lobby to the exit facing the street. She didn't run fast because of the restrictions of her skirt. She cursed her choice of outfit for the day. She called out, "Help!" as she ran.

* * *

Slayton hadn't expected the cop routine.

He spotted Iva during the confrontation with the tall coworker. Dude looked like his only goal in life was to get Iva Radler into bed. She was attractive enough to catch any man's eye, her suit unable to conceal the curvy figure beneath, but she wasn't having it and told him so. And then the "police" showed up. Thinking they might be legit, Slayton paused mid-stride.

Then the tall coworker proved himself useful. He questioned the validity of the police identification.

And the "cops" proved they were phony when one yanked a Taser and blasted the tall man into a fetal position on the floor.

Iva broke away from the second police impostor and ran.

Slayton ran, too—for the phony cops. They were turning to pursue the young woman when he reached them. A solid punch to the kidney brought one down. As his partner turned, a fast right plowed the jaw of the other. Slayton jumped over their fallen forms and ran after Iva.

9

IVA PUSHED OUT THROUGH A SWINGING GLASS DOOR AND TURNED left onto the sidewalk. Slayton followed. He ignored the commotion of witnesses but noted a security guard yelling into a radio for help. She was fifteen yards ahead. Slayton yelled her name. She looked back, but didn't stop. Her face showed fear. She wasn't going to stop for anybody. And then a heel snapped off one of her shoes.

Iva started to fall before she had a chance to face forward again. She put her arms out to soften the impact, but it was still a bad spill. Items from her purse flew across the sidewalk as she landed. Slayton reached her and blocked her slapping hands as she tried to fend him off. He didn't stop trying to get through to her.

"Iva! I'm here to help! I'm an American agent. Iva! Stop!"

He captured both of her wrists in his calloused hands.

"Iva, it's about your sister. Those two back there—"

He didn't have to explain further. The two phony cops ran toward them, shouting and shoving pedestrians out of their way. Instead of Tasers, they now carried semi-auto handguns.

Iva's eyes widened with a silent plea as she looked to Slayton for an answer.

"Come on!"

He hauled her upright. The items from her purse remained forgotten.

A gunshot—sharp, a high-pitched crack. The round burrowed into the brick wall on Iva's left. She screamed. Slayton steered her into an alley and told her to take cover. He flattened his back to the alley wall and drew his CZ P-10C from under his jacket. The pair of thugs turned into the alley.

Slayton hammered the gun across the skull of the lead man. He dropped like a sack. The other deflected Slayton's second swing and punched him in the gut. Slayton grunted, throwing his weight at the thug. They crashed into the opposite wall, punching, kicking, trying to get the upper hand on one another. Slayton twisted to one side and landed a pair of blows. He ducked a swing, then grabbed the thug's head to smack it into the wall. The second goon passed out and joined his buddy on the ground.

Slayton bent over in pain, stifling a cry, still clutching his gun. He put the pistol away and straightened with effort. Iva ran to him.

"Are you hurt?"

"We gotta go, Iva. Move!"

She followed him out of the alley, and they crossed the street against traffic. Drivers stopped short and honked at them. Slayton led Iva to his car at the curb. He was well aware the thugs had help. They'd be coming.

When he heard the racing engine of a car speeding

through traffic, he knew the help was seconds from engaging.

* * *

He opened the passenger door for Iva, and she scrambled inside. Slayton dropped behind the wheel and started the car. He almost caused another traffic collision as he executed a hasty U-turn. He wanted to get away from the enemy car as fast as possible.

He drove fast. When he passed the enemy car, he and the two backup thugs made eye contact. He kept going. They made their own frantic U-turn and began the pursuit.

Iva shouted, “What’s going on?”

“Not now!” Slayton powered through a red light and screeched the tires making a left turn.

“Tell me!”

“It’s your sister. She’s dead. I’m sorry. They think you know something.”

“What?”

“Karina was a CIA informant, and the Faction thinks she told you something.”

“How do you know she was CIA?”

“Because she worked for me, Iva. It was my job to go get her the night she died.”

Iva lapsed into shocked silence. If she’d wanted to say more, the enemy cut her off. They rammed into the back of Slayton’s car, the impact jolting them both. Slayton increased speed and weaved around other cars.

The enemy stayed close. He shouted, “Get down!” and then a salvo of submachine gun fire smacked into the car. Iva made herself small in the seat, tightening her body into a ball. More shots hit the car, but none came near him or Iva.

Slayton swerved left across the opposite lane, and then a sharp right. He turned into the parking lot of a grocery store and sped behind the building. There were fewer cars there. And no people.

“Stay down!”

Slayton rolled out of the car with the CZ P-10C clutched in both hands.

The enemy car skidded around the corner. The passenger, still half in and half out, swung his sub gun in Slayton’s direction.

Slayton fired twice. The top of the gunman’s head split, chunks of him flying away as his body fell out of the car. The body rolled in a heap of loose arms and legs before coming to a stop. The driver hit the brakes and reversed in a cloud of tire smoke. Slayton fired again, his shots punching through the windscreen. But he missed the driver. Slayton got a look at the driver’s face, though. The man was ugly. He had a face Slayton wasn’t going to forget anytime soon. The driver reversed around the corner and took off for the street once more.

Slayton stowed his gun and rejoined Iva in the car. He drove across the lot and onto another street. He drove normally, but there was nothing normal happening inside the car. Both he and Iva breathed hard, and both were shaking. Slayton regained composure first. After many years in the field, the shakes after an adrenaline rush didn’t bother him.

Iva was another story.

“Oh my god! Oh my god!”

“We’re safe.”

"Are we?" She sat up. "I thought they were going to kill me!"

"They wanted to kill *me*, Iva. Not you."

"I don't understand any of this!"

"We only have a few questions for you. Then we'll see."

"What do you mean?"

"It means you may need protection until this is over."

"I don't want to know what happened to my sister, do I?"

"No," Slayton said.

Iva lapsed into silence.

10

Slayton took Iva to a CIA safe house. It was a two-bedroom apartment in a quiet neighborhood. The Agency purchased a unit on the first floor for easy in-and-out in case of emergency.

Iva surveyed the kitchen and living room. The place was spotless with as much life as a hospital room. Very clean, bare walls, no decoration. Antiseptic was a good description. But the couches looked comfortable to her.

"How long do I need to stay here?" She removed her shoes and didn't bother to examine the broken one. She set her purse on the glass-top dining table and looked confused as she spoke to Slayton.

Slayton set his car keys on the kitchen counter and began opening cupboards. He moved fast, but Iva spotted plenty of canned goods and other items. The refrigerator was full too.

"Want a drink?" he asked. He pulled out a bottle of water. She went to the counter, and he passed her the bottle.

She would have preferred a stronger drink, but the water was cold, and the first sip tasted good. Slayton cracked open a bottle of his own.

"We're only going to ask you questions," he said, "and go from there."

"How long?"

"I don't know."

"I need clothes and a few things."

"My people can go to your apartment and get what you need. Or we can buy stuff."

"Is there a shower here?"

Slayton nodded and showed her the spacious bathroom down the hall. He also pointed out where to find the towels under the sink. He pulled the door shut when he left.

Iva stared at her reflection. She'd have to put her work clothes back on. She felt dirty all over and didn't relish the idea of wearing the outfit longer. She undressed one item at a time, putting her clothes and underwear in a pile, tossing her stockings in a wad on top. Another look in the mirror. She was shaking. Her pale skin seemed more so. Maybe it was the light. Despite how tall she was, she felt small and vulnerable. She needed to get away from her reflection fast.

She leaned into the shower and turned on the water, set the temperature, and stepped under the spray. Then she leaned against the wall and started to sob.

* * *

SLAYTON LISTENED to the water running and heard her crying.

Poor kid. And she'd face more soon...

He sat on the couch and called Mason in the US.

"What's happening, Jack?"

"I have the sister at a safe house."

"She'll be better off at the embassy."

"Staying overnight won't hurt. She has a lot to digest."

Slayton explained the fight and pursuit and how he'd delivered the news about her sister.

"You have terrific bedside manner, Jack."

"No choice," Slayton said. He took a deep breath to bury his irritation. *Pot, meet kettle.*

"I want an interview team to talk to her," Mason said. "Get her to the embassy."

"I can talk to her here, Nate. She's shaken up enough. Throwing her into a small room with a bunch of assholes won't help."

"Don't screw up."

"Your confidence inspires as usual, Nate."

"And watch your mouth, young man."

Slayton ended the call and fought the urge to toss the phone across the room. He stood and paced instead. The shower was still running. He had no plans to rush Iva, but figured she'd want clean clothes sooner rather than later. Being comfortable was key to her cooperation. He called his contact at the embassy. A team would visit Iva's apartment shortly, and Slayton said okay. The team would call when they arrived so Slayton could let them inside. He didn't want them walking in like they owned the place and spooking Iva further.

The water turned off. Ten minutes later, Iva emerged wearing her skirt and blouse. Learning clean clothes were on the way brightened her mood a little. She dropped onto one of the couches. Slayton sat on the other end.

"My boss was his usual unpleasant self," he told her.

"I'll have to move you to the embassy. It's not as nice, but it's safer. You'll have Marines protecting you there."

"Okay," she said. After a pause, she added, "I have a grumpy boss too. Oh! What do I tell them?"

"Nothing, for now."

"Are you sure?"

"It's the least of your worries right now, Iva."

"You didn't tell me your name."

"Jack. Call me Jack."

"How long have you—"

He almost laughed. Of all the questions to ask... "Almost too long," he said. "I used to be a SEAL. Got mixed up with one thing or another and took a job with my current employer. I should have stayed a civilian when I had the chance."

"Grumpy bosses make everything tough."

"My old boss and I were good friends. The new guy can be okay. Sometimes," Slayton said.

"I've been a number cruncher my whole life," she said. "My first boyfriend was my multiplication table." She smiled a little. "You know, I'm the only surviving member of my family now. Well, there's my father's sister, but she cut me off when Karina joined..." She trailed off.

"Why cut you off?"

"I didn't do enough to stop her, apparently. Karina was the stubborn one, like our mother. Once she made up her mind—"

Slayton waited. Iva didn't talk for a few moments.

Then: "Do I get to see her body at least?"

"It's better you don't."

"I need to."

Slayton nodded. "All right. I'll see about arranging it."

"What do you want to know?"

Slayton decided to start with a little history. "Tell me what you remember about how Karina joined the New Faction."

"Can you make some tea first, please?"

"I'm sorry. Of course. Hang on." Slayton left the couch and filled a kettle with water. He put it on the stove and turned on the burner. Iva came to sit at the counter. Slayton leaned against the counter edge near the stove and faced her.

"I should have thought to ask," he said.

"We both have a lot on our minds."

Slayton nodded again and remained silent. He didn't want to pressure her to answer anything. If she wanted to talk, he'd wait for her. And if tea made her comfortable enough to talk...

The kettle whistled, and he sorted through the cupboard and told her what tea they had available. She selected a bold English Breakfast. Slayton poured her a mug, and they returned to the couch.

"When do we have to go to the embassy?" she asked.

"We can go in the morning. Sleep in a nice bed tonight. I can't promise what the embassy will have for accommodations."

She looked at her steaming tea. "Well, you wanted to know—"

"Uh-huh."

"Karina met a few friends in college who were real anti-authority types. She was bored, so one night she went to a meeting with them, which turned out to be a recruiting effort for what became the New Red Army..."

Karina didn't join right away, Iva explained. She

attended more meetings, learned their philosophy, and identified with what they termed as "modern class warfare."

"They talked about how wages stay stagnant while cost of living goes up, and there's no way to live unless you're in the one percent. And nobody can get there because corporations want to create a slave class they can keep in perpetual debt. She bought into it because our parents always struggled. Neither finished college. Dad started a business, but wasn't good at it. They were always a day late and a Euro short no matter how hard they worked."

Karina, Iva continued, soon realized most families lived the same way, and began to resent those who had the coveted jobs, the connections, the privilege, others didn't. She developed radical ideas on how to solve the problem, ideas encouraged by her new friends. The only way to fix the problem was to tear down the existing system. The only way to tear down the existing system meant bullets and bombs because ballots didn't work.

"So, she joined and left everything behind to go all-in as a member of the team," Iva concluded.

"I see."

"But you said—you said she became an informant?"

Slayton nodded. "Do you know about a man named Hans?"

"No."

"Another cell member. They were lovers. Later, Hans became a suspect when a mission went sour and weapons disappeared. They thought he was a traitor who sold them out to the BKA and lined his own pockets by selling their guns on the side. They murdered him. Karina swore he didn't do anything wrong and turned to us to get revenge."

She sipped her tea. "I had no idea."

"She broke off all contact?"

"Not all. I heard from her now and then. She surprised me with a visit sometimes."

"Did she see you in the last few days?"

"Actually, yes," Iva said.

"Did she give you anything? Tell you to look somewhere specific if anything ever happened to her?"

"No. I wish she had. But maybe—"

"What?"

"She gave me a picture of us. From when we were teenagers. We'd taken a holiday with my parents. The last one before Dad died, now that I think about it. She told me it was a copy from her collection, and she wanted me to have it. Put it in a nice frame, too."

"Where's the picture now?"

"On my wall. We're in bikinis on the deck of a boat."

"We need the picture, Iva. She may have put something in the frame."

"Why don't I give you my key—"

"Once I activate the security system, you can't go out."

"You think I want to go anywhere else after today?"

Slayton figured she didn't.

* * *

ANOTHER CALL to his embassy contact revealed nobody had gone to Iva's to get her clothes yet. Slayton suggested they stand down. Since he was going, he could grab her stuff. He set the alarm system and told her any breach would trigger a response team who would rush to the place. She said she only wanted to go to bed, so he showed her one of the guest rooms, set the security system, and departed.

Slayton hoped traffic wasn't too bad. He wanted to hurry. Leaving Iva alone too long wasn't a good idea. At least she'd be safe at the "safe" house. He was certain the Faction didn't know of its existence. But he still drove with urgency because he'd been certain they didn't know about Karina either. He hoped Iva's picture provided the clue they needed. He wanted to know what Karina would have told him had she not been murdered.

11

Markus Frenz wasn't happy.

He and a crew of four other operatives trashed Iva's apartment the same as they had Karina's. So far, they'd found nothing Karina might have left her sister. He began to wonder, as he stepped through the debris, if he'd miscalculated. But the CIA had the same idea. Had they been there first?

Frenz kicked aside a shredded couch cushion and stepped over the remains of a broken table. His eyes moved left, right, looking for anything his men had missed. It wasn't until he spotted Iva's collection of family photos on a wall did he find the proper spark of inspiration. The same inspiration he had at Karina's. Why hadn't he started there?

Nobody had searched the photos yet. His men had moved from the living room and kitchen to the two bedrooms and hall closet. He scanned each picture, then started on the left side. He tore each picture out of the frame and tossed the parts on the floor if he found nothing hidden. The last picture revealed what he wanted.

But Frenz leered at it first. It was the original photo of Karina and Iva as bikini-clad teenagers on the deck of a boat. He broke the picture out of the frame. Inside, he found the square-folded sheet of paper wedged behind the picture. Taking the folded sheet, he discarded the frame.

Jackpot.

He unfolded the sheet and saw the note across the top. *Get this to the American embassy if anything happens to me.*

The page showed a list of names.

The names of the leaders of the New Red Army Faction.

And Alexandra Ruhl's name topped the list.

The names below Alexandra's included the cream of the crop in EU leaders, the tech sector, major CEOs, all of whom supported Alexandra's effort.

"I found it!" Frenz announced. He called his men to him, and they emerged from the bedrooms. He showed them the list, then folded it and slipped the sheet of paper into a pocket. Alexandra could have the list. He planned to keep the photo for himself.

Frenz was about to say more when he heard a key turning in the dead bolt.

* * *

SLAYTON STEPPED off the elevator with relief. The motor and running gear made a terrible clunking noise on ascent.

He turned left and walked along the well-lit hall. Overhead fluorescent lights buzzed. The alcoves of each apartment had individual circular lights highlighting the entry. The brown carpet wasn't dirty or frayed at the edges. The white paint along the wall looked spotless. The usual German efficiency was on display.

Slayton fished Iva's key from his left pocket and stopped at her door. He bent to examine the lock and frowned. No sign of careless scratches from an overeager lock picker. But it didn't mean the apartment was empty. He put his ear to the door and listened. A man was talking inside. Slayton couldn't make out all the words, but the voice wasn't coming from the TV or radio.

Slayton kept the key in his left hand. He took out his CZ P-10C with his right and slipped his index finger through the trigger guard. Firearms instructors taught never to touch the trigger until you were sure of a target. Slayton was sure plenty of targets waited behind the door.

He inserted the key and turned back the deadbolt. He did the same with the knob and heard the distinct *click* of the lock tripping. Slayton turned the knob, gave the door a push, and stepped left, out of the alcove. He waited at the wall. The CZ 9mm warmed in his grip.

The door swung inward on squeaky hinges, stopping partway. Slayton waited. No sounds beyond the door now. The talking ceased. Fingers grabbed at the inner edge of the door, opened it more—

And then a face. A blue-eyed blond man with glasses and a handgun. The roar of the CZ 9mm bounced off the narrow hallway walls. The slug took part of the blond man's face away, bloody chunks of flesh decorating the wall behind, leaving bloody and jagged bone visible. The corpse collapsed. Men started yelling. Slayton moved from the left side of the alcove to the right and began retreating backward one step at a time. He kept his gun aimed at the alcove.

Another gunman emerged, but he looked left first instead of the other way. He expected Slayton to remain in one spot. Slayton fired again. The 9mm hollow points burrowed into the back of the gunman's head and out his nose like a 147-grain booger. Slayton didn't have a chance to feel pleased with his shooting performance. Two more gunners exited, and this time they turned in the correct direction. They rushed at Slayton, bent low, screaming. Slayton fired but missed, then they were on him.

Goon One had thick arms and legs, and his middle was just as wide and solid. He held no gun and came at Slayton with open hands.

Goon Two wasn't as big, and Slayton saw him going for a weapon.

Goon One plowed into Slayton. Breath left him as he landed on the floor and felt a sharp blow to his ribs as the goon struck with one of his hands. The second goon yelled for his partner to get out of the way, but the big guy wasn't giving up the kill.

With little space in the hallway, Slayton had to work fast and make his hits count. He kept a tight grip on the P-10C and swung it at the big man's head. It was the best option, as Goon One rose to his knees, while also raising a fist for an attack. The autoloader arced in his direction, then it stopped. Slayton's right arm ran into the brick wall of the big man's left arm, and he pummeled at Slayton's face with his right fist. The hits hurt, stung deep—once, twice. Slayton struck back, holding his gun to the side and jamming the muzzle into the goon's throat. Goon One choked and pulled back. Slayton fired—blood and bits of flesh sprayed back at him, but there was no other option. Goon One began to slump, and Slayton shoved him away. Doing so freed up the shot Goon Two wanted. Slayton shot him in the face before he fired. Goon Two crumpled to the carpet as Slayton struggled to his feet and searched for another threat.

Yet another figure ran from Iva's apartment. He fired twice at Slayton, who hit the deck again as the shots peppered the walls. The shooter sprinted down the hall away from Slayton. From his prone position, Slayton fired once. He missed.

Slayton tried to get up again, using the wall for support. Another apartment door behind him opened. A man began yelling. Slayton walked like Frankenstein, trying to force away the pain in his face and ribs. He shouted back for the man to call for help. Then Slayton found a reserve of strength. He ran after the last man, though not fast enough, and with more of a shuffle than steady run. Because the man's face finally registered. He was the ugly man in the car who'd chased him and Iva.

He had to know what the enemy found. The entire mission depended on the information.

Slayton tried to run faster.

12

Markus Frenz flinched as splinters from the doorframe pelted his face. But the bullet missed him. He slammed through the stairwell door and started down the steps.

He wasn't sure if the American recognized him, but he recognized the American. They'd have their showdown very soon. Getting the list back to Alexandra was top priority. As much as he wanted to take on the American *now*, his own mission came first.

Frenz turned down one flight, taking the stairs fast. Down another and another still. Then he opened the door to a hall, closed the door, and waited. He was going to let the American pass. He watched the stairwell through a square window. And hoped the door concealed him enough for the American not to notice.

He waited, casting furtive glances back along the hall to make sure nobody was coming his way. Then the American came stomping down the stairwell, leaning on the rail. He turned and continued down the next flight.

Frenz let out a breath. He wanted to go behind the

American and shoot him in the back. But he had to get the list to Alexandra. He moved away from the door and hurried to the opposite end of the hall. From there, he used the elevator. He'd end up further from his car than he wanted, but cops would be rushing to the scene after the shooting. He might have a better chance of slipping through their net if he stayed on foot.

Dropping his gun, spare mags, and holster on the elevator car floor, he exited the building via a side door. The quiet sidewalk and street greeted him, but loud sirens grew in volume. He started walking. If any police officers stopped him, at least he wasn't carrying any weapons.

* * *

Slayton stumbled onto the concrete outside the main entrance. Lights shone on him. He looked into the bright lights and the Berlin cops racing to him. He glanced at the gun in his right hand.

Oh, shit.

They began shouting at him to drop the gun. He didn't have to hear the command in English to understand. Slayton let the CZ fall to the ground and raised his arms. Nothing to do but surrender. He'd find a way out after a phone call or two.

But he was in trouble, and he knew it. There'd be much more than a lecture from Nathan Mason this time.

* * *

The party was in full swing, and Alexandra Ruhl couldn't have been happier.

She'd packed her Berlin penthouse with food and guests. A charismatic DJ provided the music. Alexandra was, of course, looking for donations to her charity. It was not a secret. In return for the generosity of her guests, she provided a good time. She'd opened wide the French doors to her three balconies. No guest lacked anything. All had dressed to kill.

Alexandra wore a slinky party dress which hugged every curve and showed off a low neckline she didn't bother to conceal. She'd made the rounds multiple times, working her sales pitch. Now, she stood at a wall near a large painting, taking a break, sipping on a martini. She'd made sure to stay extra busy because Frenz and his team were at work. She didn't want to dwell on the state of their progress, or what it meant if Frenz failed to find anything.

Her stoic expression broadened into a big smile when a dark-haired man in his fifties stepped her way. "Alexandra," he said, "I'm sorry to be so late." He was Frank Rosen, an American, an old friend of her late husband, her lover, and a member of the New Red Army Faction. He was part of the command council. He ran his own billionaire empire in the United States—focused on oil and gasoline with a growing reach into renewable energy research, big pharma, and crypto.

"What kept you?" she asked, leaning in for a kiss. He planted one on her left cheek. She squeezed his right arm. It was the extent of her affection when others were around. She still held the martini in her left hand.

"I was on the phone putting out fires. You know, the usual emergencies." They had to speak loudly over the music. Rosen took the martini from her and set it on an end table against the wall. "Let's dance." He took her hand and led her away.

Alexandra didn't argue and liked his take-charge attitude. They'd begun their affair prior to her husband's death. She had never felt bad about it. Her late elderly husband could never satisfy her, little blue pills or not. Frank? Total opposite. They danced close, his grip gentle but firm, and they communicated with their eyes. It was a silent exchange only the two of them understood. Alexandra often felt lonely despite the number of people around her. It was why the charity and her extracurricular activities played such a large role in her life.

But when Frank was with her...

She felt warm being near him and didn't mind how the tight party dress restricted leg movement. She followed his lead as smoothly as possible. The song ended, and Frank wanted a drink. Alexandra was happy for a pause. When she caught the eye of Markus Frenz in the entryway, she told Frank to get his drink. She had to take care of a little business.

* * *

Alexandra took Frenz to the side of the entryway where a corner wall blocked them from view.

"You found something?" she asked.

Frenz nodded and explained the search and fight at the apartment. The police could not connect the dead or wounded crew members to her, but she regretted their loss. Frenz showed her the list he found, and Alexandra examined the names with alarm.

"We came dangerously close—"

"To losing everything," he completed. "For sure."

She folded the paper and slipped it under the top of the dress against her left breast. "Good work, Markus. Now we need to find the American agent and the sister."

"Working on it."

"They may have the sister in custody."

"I'll call our sources at the embassy and see. They haven't reported anything yet."

She nodded and gestured to the entryway elevator to dismiss him. Frenz departed. She waited until the doors slid shut, then returned to the party with a big smile. She wanted to duck into her bedroom with Frank and celebrate the victory without anybody else around.

* * *

SLAYTON SAT on a gurney in the ER with a police guard two feet away. The nurse had closed a curtain to conceal him, but not because of the cop. Everybody in the ER received the courtesy. But conversations between patients and medical staff were easy to hear. The curtain hung on a U-shaped rail.

They'd plugged him into a blood pressure monitor and a quiet medic examined his injuries. He told Slayton, "You'll live," and then left Slayton alone with the police guard.

His face and body hurt, but he knew he wasn't in terrible shape. He'd be back in action shortly, unless the cops put him through the wringer. What he wanted to know was who was coming to get him. He'd alerted the embassy, but they had to deal with the locals, too. Considering Slayton decided *not* to visit the BKA as ordered upon his arrival, he knew the locals would resist his continued presence.

The curtain moved back, and two people entered. A man and a woman. Slayton tried to keep his eyes off the woman. The man gave the cop the order to leave, and the officer departed. The man faced Slayton and flashed a BKA identification.

"Mr. Slayton? I'm Rolf Gerheardt. This is my associate, Kara Botticker."

Slayton noticed Kara Botticker didn't produce any identification.

Gerheardt cut an impressive figure in his gray suit, his face lean and chin prominent. Dark hair, close-cropped, touched with gray.

Kara Botticker was a blonde with typical German blue eyes. She examined Slayton like an exterminator plotting to poison a termite colony. Curious, yet detached.

Gerheardt continued talking.

"We expected you to visit us, per the instructions of Mr. Mason."

"Whoops," Slayton said.

"You will come with us then."

"Okay." Slayton was in no position to argue.

Slayton waited for the silent medic to unplug him so he could sign out. Gerheardt instructed the cop to return Slayton's belongings. Then Slayton followed the German agents out of the ER. He walked behind Gerheardt, with Kara Botticker behind him. He had a feeling the rest of their interaction wasn't going to be any more cordial than how it started.

13

THEY DROVE SLAYTON TO BKA HEADQUARTERS IN THE MITTE district, center of Berlin. Every building in the complex appeared the same. Concrete squares with row after row of triangular windows. No frills German efficiency.

Gerheardt and the silent Kara brought him into a conference room. He sat down. They sat near him. Gerheardt did the talking.

"You've left a dead body or two in your wake, Mr. Slayton."

Slayton wondered if Kara was mute.

"We should expel you posthaste," Gerheardt added.

Slayton finally said, "Have my people been in touch?"

"Yes."

"And?"

"You have a lot of explaining to do."

"You're aware of the basics," Slayton said. He went through a rundown of Karina Radler and the New Red Army Faction anyway. The two Gérmans listened without comment. Slayton ended with details about Iva, and why he went to her apartment. “They attacked me,” he concluded, pointing at his face, “and I defended myself.”

“If you knew they were behind the door, you should have stood down.”

“Don’t tell me my business, Agent Gerheardt.”

“Don’t shoot up German domiciles, Mr. Slayton.”

Said Kara.

Slayton reacted with mock surprise. “Wow. You’re not mute.”

Her face soured. Somebody knocked at the door. Gerheardt left his chair to answer while Slayton and Kara stared at each other without a hint of friendship or cooperation.

“Your compatriots, Mr. Slayton,” Gerheardt announced. He led three more men into the room. They were CIA people from the embassy and Slayton knew one of them. Gordon Kealey, his local contact. Slayton’s mood lightened with the presence of the home team. They sat on his side of the table, and Kealey told Slayton not to talk.

Slayton grinned at Kara. Her face remained impassive.

Kealey said, “The CIA apologizes for this incident.”

“We understand problems happen,” Gerheardt said, “but now we have a bigger issue. We have to somehow explain what happened.”

“A fight between criminal gangs ought to satisfy,” Kealey said. “We’ll even draft the statement if you’d like.”

Kara muttered, “America *always* has the answers.”

“There’s no reason to make this difficult,” Kealey said. “Our mission against these terrorists isn’t finished.”

“We’ll be active from now on,” Gerheardt said. “Mr. Slayton will work with us.”

"You?" Slayton asked Gerheardt.

"Me," Kara answered.

"Oh. Great."

Kealey said, "I need to talk to Mr. Slayton's superior. Can we get back to you in twenty-four hours?"

"Satisfactory," Gerheardt said.

"All right." Kealey turned to Slayton. "You ready?"

"As soon as I get my stuff back."

Gerheardt pushed Slayton's bundle across the table to him.

* * *

SLAYTON SAT in back of the embassy car with Kealey. The other two CIA officers sat up front.

Kealey said, "Mason isn't happy."

"Not news. When is Mason *ever* happy?"

Kealey didn't answer.

"I'll deal with the Old Buzzard," Slayton said. "Right now, I need to get back to the safe house. Iva Radler is alone, and I'm sure freaking out because I've been gone so long. If the other side found anything, they're going to destroy it, but Iva will still be a target."

"What did she tell you?"

Slayton explained the "gift" of the picture.

"Did she look inside the frame?"

"She did not," Slayton answered. "She has no idea if there's anything there. But the other side doesn't know that."

"Me and Hawkins and Grant," Kealey said, gesturing at the two men up front, "will stay the night with you and the woman. You need the backup. Tomorrow morning, we all go to the embassy and do this the right way."

Slayton wanted to disagree, but decided it was best not to argue this time.

"The three of you need to keep your distance, though," he told them. "She's touchy enough."

"We'll stay in the background," Kealey assured him.

The ride continued, and Slayton turned to look out the window. The passing scenery hardly registered. Iva still needed clothes, he realized. He'd failed at both tasks he'd set out to do. And now the enemy was two steps ahead. Slayton had to reverse the odds fast before they won the whole game.

* * *

Slayton punched the entry code into the touchpad beside the door. The lock popped. But only the electronic lock. He used the embassy-issued key for the knob and deadbolt. The code also deactivated the security systems. He entered without any danger of the alarms going off. Kealey and the other two embassy-based CIA men followed Slayton inside.

Iva came at him in a rush, throwing her arms around his neck. "I'm so glad you came back!" Slayton almost lost his balance. He awkwardly hugged her in return and then she pulled away. She blinked in surprise at the presence of the other three.

"Who are these men?"

Slayton introduced Kealey, Hawkins, and Grant. "They're backup in case of an emergency. And they'll escort us to the embassy in the morning."

"What about my clothes?"

Slayton cleared his throat and pulled back the corners of his mouth in an embarrassed grin. He told her what occurred at her apartment and added it was the reason for his long delay.

"Terrific!" she exclaimed, pivoting and marching back into the living room. The CIA men followed behind. "What now?" she yelled, turning to face Slayton, but ignoring the others.

"We can get what you need in the morning," he said. "It's only one night."

She cursed and turned to look out a window.

Slayton gave Kealey, Hawkins, and Grant a tour of the place. There were only two bedrooms so the embassy officers would have to sleep on the couches. Kealey sorted through the kitchen, found it lacking, and sent Hawkins and Grant for a list of supplies. He said they all needed something decent to eat before bed as well as a proper breakfast in the morning. Iva didn't seem to care. She stared out the window with her lips in a tight line.

Slayton sat on the couch facing the television and flipped channels. He wanted to see if he could find a program to fill the silence. Nobody talked much after Kealey cooked a late dinner. Later, he and Hawkins and Grant played gin and kept their voices down. Slayton and Iva watched TV with Iva on a couch by herself. She sat with her legs crossed and arms folded and not even a popular sitcom cracked her angry façade.

Kealey and his men decided to sleep in shifts. Slayton and Iva retreated to their bedrooms. Slayton undressed and stretched out under the covers and hoped for a decent night's sleep after such a hectic day. He dozed off after a few minutes, then snapped awake. His brain was still busy. And a subconscious thought fought its way to the surface.

Why hadn't the embassy sent a woman with Kealey to help with Iva?

14

KEALEY, AS PROMISED, PREPARED BREAKFAST THE NEXT MORNING.

Slayton finished first and excused himself from the table to call headquarters.

“Everything all right, Jack?” Mason answered. The boss was working very late.

Slayton concealed his surprise.

“For now,” Slayton replied.

“I’ve been up half the night wondering about a few things,” Mason said. “How did the opposition know about Karina and the pick-up site?”

“She screwed up somewhere, is my guess. They tortured her for the information. The sister was easy to think of, too. I don’t think there’s a leak.”

“We may have to let the Germans take the lead now,” Mason continued. “Only assist as needed.”

“They’ll push us out, and you know it.”

“I’m aware. And you may be right. Do you think the sister has anything more we can use?”

“I hope so. We’ll find out.”

"We need *something* to stay in the game. And *results,* Jack."

"I'll get results."

"Get back in touch when you have an update."

Mason hung up before Slayton said okay.

* * *

MASON SLEPT on his office couch instead of going home. The telephone ringing on his desk woke him. He sat up. His suit was rumpled, he was groggy, and he looked like hell. The phone kept ringing. His joints creaked and popped as he forced himself up and went to pick up the phone.

"Yes?"

"It's Reema. Did you forget our meeting?"

Mason cursed. "I need a few minutes." He hung up the phone.

I'm going to spend the rest of the day playing catch-up.

As an old spymaster, late nights and office couches weren't unfamiliar. He had necessities in place for such occasions. Especially in recent years, since his wife passed. He pulled a shaving kit from the bottom drawer of his desk and headed for the men's room. He felt the eyes of the bullpen watching him, but he didn't acknowledge.

* * *

REEMA ASHRAF PACED in the conference room while the other four managers of Z Section sat at the long table. She looked sharp in her slacks and blue blouse. She wore a silver necklace Slayton gave her. It was a present for her last birthday.

She'd tied back her long black hair in a ponytail. She couldn't get Slayton off her mind.

Reema found herself more and more preoccupied with Jack when he was in harm's way. The "mission" had separated them once before. She didn't want it to happen again. Reema traced her anxiety to her three-year ordeal still present in her subconscious.

The four at the table talked in hushed tones, but she tuned them out. They weren't talking about work, and she wasn't in the mood for casual chit-chat. Reema was also concerned about Nathan Mason. The Old Buzzard had nothing in his life but work. It was quite obvious to her he'd slept at the office. He was trying to fill the void in his life with the job, and she didn't think it was helping his state of mind.

Finally, the conference room door swung open, and Nathan Mason entered in a rush.

"Sorry for the delay," he announced.

Reema took her seat as Mason stood at the head of the table and began the meeting.

* * *

Mason let out a heavy breath as he set his files and agenda folder on the table. He'd brushed his teeth and performed a very quick GI shower in the men's room but hadn't had time to shave. His suit was still wrinkled. He hoped they didn't ask questions.

"We have a man in the field who needs anything we can discover. We thought we had the lead to end all leads regarding the New Red Army Faction, but we lost our asset. Now we need to dig through our data and look for another thread, something our man in Berlin can use to find the top dog, the leader of the group, who will connect us to Andreas Ritter. Our goal remains the same. Kill the snake. Any questions?"

His people remained silent. Mason glanced at Reema Ashraf at the opposite end of the table. She smiled with encouragement. Mason began to feel better. If he had Reema in his corner, he couldn't have screwed up too much or looked like a bum who'd slept in an alley.

"All right," he said, "get to work. Move it."

His staff scattered from the conference room like a cluster of pigeons chasing breadcrumbs. But Reema didn't leave her seat. When the door shut, she spoke.

"Are you okay, Nathan?"

"No," Mason answered. He lowered his head. "Rough night. I slept in the office."

"I can tell."

"It gets tough sometimes, Reema."

"What does?"

"Being alone. Going home to an empty house." He raised his head to look at her. "Losing a spouse is horrible. I hope you never—"

He stopped. She waited.

"Never what?" she asked.

"I don't mean to presume with you and Jack, and you know I don't approve of workplace relationships. But considering what the two of you have already been through...don't wait any longer than you have to."

She smiled again, gathered her folders, and left the room. Mason watched her go and felt silly. Not everybody could identify with him. He was foolish to think so. He had more years behind him than ahead, and his point of view didn't match the young people's. They didn't understand. Yet.

But he felt good about the meeting. Short, sweet, to the point. Now he had to wait to see what his staff discovered. In the meantime, he had other tasks to tend to. Like going home for a proper shower and change of clothes. On his way out, he told Reema he wouldn't be gone long and to take over till he returned.

15

REEMA KNOCKED ON MASON'S DOOR THREE HOURS LATER. SHE held two file folders and a notebook. Mason waved her inside.

"What did we find?" he asked.

"Two names," Reema announced. She sat in front of Mason's desk and crossed her legs. The boss looked much better. He'd shaved and put on a blue suit in place of the darker one from the day before. She placed the file folders on the desk. Mason took the one on top and opened it as Reema consulted her notes. "They're both money men suspected of laundering funds for extremist groups. They may hold the keys we're looking for. Danish banker Niklas Kragh and a Swiss banker named Jude Garvin." She looked up. Mason donned a pair of gold-rimmed bifocals as he read. He was looking at Kragh's file.

"Hmmm," Mason said. He scanned the pages and stopped and frowned. "We have an asset with Kragh?"

"She hasn't provided much, and she's been with him almost a year," Reema said.

"Why did we place her with Kragh?"

"You'd have to ask Special Activities, she's their bird," Reema said. "We suspect Kragh of laundering money and investing funds. He then funnels the money to terrorists. I think he is our best bet."

"Any solid connection to the New Faction?"

"He's handled the funds for a shell company we've connected to low-level members of the Faction."

"And this other one. Garvin?" Mason traded one file for the other. He paged through. "Any connection with him?"

"Same as Kragh."

Mason eyed her over the rim of his glasses. "This is weak, Reema. This is chasing our tail."

"It's worth applying pressure to see if they know anything. They may know somebody who does. They're part of that world, Nathan."

"What would you do in my place?" he asked.

"Assign a stalker team to each, make sure they notice, spook them a little. If they make any moves, redirect Jack to intercept. He's probably done everything he can in Berlin now anyway."

Mason removed his glasses and sat back. He let out a breath. She waited. He stared past her, glancing once through the glass wall to watch the activity in the bullpen.

"All right," he said. "We'll watch them and see. Jack's got more to do in Berlin, I think, but I agree our effort there has a time limit." He slid the folders back to her. "Get it going."

Reema took the files and departed.

* * *

Since Kealey did the cooking, Slayton and Iva did the cleaning. They washed the pans and plates in the sink. Slayton took extra time with the pans to make sure they were spotless. Kealey suggested calling the embassy for another car. He didn't want the five of them to force themselves into one. Hawkins and Grant could take the other car and act as security. Slayton agreed.

Iva appeared anxious. Slayton took her aside while Kealey called the embassy.

"You all right?"

"Just this." She pulled at her blouse. "I'm wearing day-old clothes, you know?"

"I get it."

She said, "I'll be glad when we're done. I really don't know—"

Kealey called out, "We're all set."

Iva's face drained of color as she looked over Slayton's shoulder. He turned. Then Iva screamed...

* * *

Slayton didn't know why Kealey and the other two embassy officers had pistols in their hands. All he knew was the pistols had suppressors attached, and they were aiming the guns at him and Iva.

He yelled for her to get down. They stood near the dining table close to the kitchen. Kealey and his men were mere feet away, near the couches and television. A bullet from Kealey's autoloader tugged at Slayton's jacket as he hauled out the CZ 9mm from his shoulder harness. He dived for the dining table, using his left hand to push it up and over. The table landed with a thud on its opposite edge.

Two rounds chunked into the light wood. Slayton had a clear shot at Grant around the right side. He took it, firing a two-round burst, tagging Grant in the center of his chest. The impact of the 9mm slugs turned his white shirt red, and he fell to the floor. Slayton's unsuppressed return fire thundered in the small space. He shifted to the left side and winged a shot at Kealey as he dived behind the couch facing Slayton. Slayton fired through the back of the couch, his string of rapid shots ripping through the cushions. He raised his aim to take off the top of Hawkins's exposed head as the other embassy man tried to shoot back.

Slayton ducked and reloaded. No more shots came his way. He eased around the left end of the table, the CZ extended in his right hand, and approached the couch. When he reached the other side, he found Kealey stretched out on the floor. Blood pooled beneath him and red holes dotted his shirt. His eyes remained open, but he was dead.

"Who did you call, Kealey?" Slayton said out loud. He hurried to search the dead man's body for his phone, pulling it from the right pocket of Kealey's pants. Examining the last number dialed, he frowned. It was a local call, but not a number associated with the US embassy. Slayton put the phone in his own pocket and went to check on Iva.

He found her behind the kitchen counter, on the floor, her face panic-stricken and her eyes wide. But she wasn't hurt.

"Come on." He hauled her up.

"What—" she stammered. "Why?"

"I think I know."

He pushed her ahead toward the door. One thought was clear in his mind. He now knew who told the New Red Army Faction about Karina.

* * *

Slayton drove fast. Iva sat low in the passenger seat, still breathing hard, as if she'd run a 10K.

"Embassy?" she asked.

"What?"

"Are we going to the embassy like we planned?"

"Not safe. If it's been penetrated by the New Faction, they'll try again."

"Then where are we going?"

"I have friends in the BKA."

The answer satisfied her. She asked no more questions. Slayton knew calling Rolf Gerheardt a *friend* was stretching the truth, but it wasn't a detail Iva needed to know.

The number on Kealey's phone...

Slayton pulled into a shopping center parking lot and used his phone to call Mason. Iva sat up. Her eyes bounced back and forth as she tried to keep watch on everything going on around her.

"Jack?" Mason answered.

"It's bad, Nate." Slayton related the shooting at the safe house. "I need a number traced. The last one Kealey dialed. It might be the only lead we have."

"Read it to me."

Slayton did so.

"I'll start a trace," Mason said. "What about the sister?"

"She's with me."

"Where are you going?"

"Not telling."

"Jack—"

Slayton hung up and put the phone away. He drove back into traffic.

He glared at Iva. She was watching him. Slayton turned to keep his eyes on the road. He had no words for her. Nothing with which to reassure her. He wasn't feeling very sure of himself. The enemy was winning. He had to score a victory, or the mission to stop the New Faction and capture or kill Andreas Ritter would go up in smoke. And Iva didn't deserve to have a target on her back. He needed to remove the threat to her and do so fast. He hadn't been able to protect Karina, but he *might* be able to protect Iva.

But he needed help.

He hoped Rolf and Kara at the BKA could provide the necessary assistance. While he went hunting.

16

SLAYTON SAT ALONE IN A CONFERENCE ROOM AT BKA headquarters. Rolf and the tall blonde, Kara Botticker, spoke with Iva in another room. The cup of tea Slayton asked for had gone cold, but remained on the otherwise bare table before him. They'd left him alone, and he tried not to feel like the walls were closing in on him. But every now and then, he sensed the room getting smaller.

His phone rang. He looked. The screen displayed Mason's name. Slayton answered.

"Where are you, young man?" Mason demanded.

"With Gerheardt at the BKA."

"Good thinking. We got a hit on the number."

"Go."

"It belongs to a man named Markus Frenz. Ring a bell?"

"Karina mentioned him in a report. He was the man who murdered her lover."

"You better share this with Rolf rather than pursuing him yourself."

"Sounds like an order."

"I'm not making a suggestion, Jack." Mason hung up.

Slayton put away his phone with a grin on his face. Mason enjoyed hanging up first.

He checked his watch, anxious to get back in action. Now he needed to talk to Rolf and Kara. He hoped they didn't keep him waiting much longer.

* * *

SLAYTON WAITED in the quiet room longer indeed. He wondered what Reema was doing and if she was keeping busy. He didn't like being away from her, but the job required him to be gone sometimes. As long as he came back...but he didn't like to think about not coming back.

No sound from outside the conference room leaked in, so he didn't hear Rolf and Kara until Rolf pushed open the door. The pair stepped inside. The sudden noise of the door opening jolted Slayton from his daydreaming.

"You didn't finish your tea," Rolf Gerheardt pointed out. He and the tall blonde sat opposite. Kara frowned at the CIA man.

"It got cold," Slayton said.

"We can warm it up, if you like."

"How long are you planning to keep me here, Rolf?"

"Only long enough to figure out where Markus Frenz is hiding. We have a team tracking him now."

"Are you forcing me out?"

"No. But Kara will go with you."

Slayton turned to her. "Do you ever smile?"

She said, "On Sundays. For five minutes."

"Are you sure that's not nine minutes too long?"

Gerheardt slapped the tabletop. "Enough. Jack, it's a

favor from me and my superiors that you're going anywhere. I *should* send you home."

"I understand."

"Now, about Iva Radler. We don't think she knows anything helpful, but we will have to keep her in protective custody for the time being."

"Okay. As long as she's safe."

"What do you intend to do as we continue?" the German asked.

"I want a few minutes with this Frenz fellow. I'd like to be close when we break the New Faction."

"Will you behave?"

"I will."

"Good! Let's talk about Mr. Frenz..."

* * *

NO WORD FROM KEALEY. Too much time had passed, Frenz realized. Something had gone wrong. Slayton survived. And the woman. Which meant what? Where would he take Iva Radler now?

Markus Frenz sat in an empty bar with a beer, on a stool in front of the bar itself. The owner was a friend and comrade-in-arms. He let Frenz sit and wait while tending to his tasks. The bar wasn't open yet.

Frenz watched his phone. He'd placed it before him, but the screen refused to light up with Kealey's call. There was no sense in waiting any longer. Slayton and the woman remained alive, and Frenz hadn't even asked the location of the safe house. He couldn't send a team to check or go see himself. By now, the CIA would have cleaned up the bodies and the mess. And if they were tracing Kealey's phone calls—

The idea forced Frenz from his meandering thoughts. He had to get rid of his phone. There was only one way.

"You all right, Markus?"

Frenz looked down the bar where the owner, a man named Klaus, leaned halfway out of a doorway.

"You made a sound like you were hurt," Klaus said.

"Just thought of a problem," Frenz answered. He wasn't aware of making any noise.

"Anything I can do?"

"Bring me a bucket of water."

"There is a sink on the other side of the bar in front of you. Will that work?"

"Perfect."

Frenz left the barstool and went around the bar. Inserting the stopper in the drain, Frenz turned on the faucet. Water hissed from the spout and filled the deep sink.

"Markus—"

"Nothing for you to worry about, Klaus."

Frenz dropped his phone into the water.

"My goodness—"

"I don't want them to trace me. *You* don't want me traced *here*."

"I suppose not. What's happening?"

Frenz explained while the smartphone sank to the bottom of the sink. What he didn't tell Klaus was he hoped he shorted out the phone in time.

But even if he'd stopped the CIA and BKA from tracking his phone, he remained at risk. They could still link the number Kealey dialed to him and find him the old-fashioned way. Which gave Frenz a little more time. But only a little.

He had to alert Alexandra and vanish. *Fast.*

* * *

"What phone are you using now?"

"I bought a burner." Frenz spoke as he drove. He'd connected the phone to the car's Bluetooth. He told her everything, she listened without comment, then asked her question.

"What are your plans?"

"The less you know, the better. But I'm getting out of Germany until further notice."

"Don't go near Andreas."

"I will not," Frenz interrupted. "But I'm also not calling anybody else. You will need to send out the alert."

"Already doing so."

"Okay."

"You messed up, Markus."

"I did more than mess up, Alexandra."

"But our CIA friends messed up more. All three were at the safe house?"

"Yes. Kealey told me they were all there. And we're assuming Kealey didn't scramble his phone log or protect it some other way."

"They'd still crack it, though. At least you have a head start."

"I need to go. I'll get word to you somehow, once I'm able."

"Good luck," Alexandra said.

"To all of us."

Frenz pushed a button on the steering wheel to disconnect the call. Then he pounded a fist on the wheel. Running and hiding wasn't his idea of a good time. It was a waste of his training and intelligence. But he had to think of the rest of the organization. If they all went down, who'd remain to carry on the war?

He drove home and hurried to pack as much as he could. Money wasn't a concern. He had access to the reserve accounts to meet basic needs. His mind raced to list places he could go. And when he reached his destination, he needed to get rid of the car. Frenz wanted nothing the enemy might trace to him. High technology was great. It enabled the New Red Army Faction, but the enemy had high-tech toys, too. Devices worked for and against the cause. The trick was to know how the enemy could leverage technology against them and plan to thwart the effort.

Suitcases packed. Time to go.

As soon as he drove out of the underground garage below the building, he spotted the BKA car.

He'd get his fight after all.

Frenz smiled as he pressed on the accelerator.

17

An hour earlier, with their plan to find Frenz squared away, Slayton visited with Iva Radler one more time.

He wasn't certain he'd see her again.

"What are they going to do with me?" she asked.

Slayton frowned. "Nobody told you?"

Iva shook her head.

Slayton cursed under his breath. This was no way to treat a witness, and Gerheardt knew better.

The German Feds had her in a small "interview room" with no windows and only a table and chair. It was where they spoke to suspects. The room was not friendly or comfortable. The chairs, fashioned out of metal, were cold and hard, and the walls bare and white.

"Protective custody for now. Don't worry," he added, gesturing around the room, "it will be better than this."

"If you say so."

Iva looked defeated. There was no light in her eyes. And Slayton wasn't sure how to reassure her. He decided to tell her what they had planned. He told her they were going after the man who murdered her sister.

"Then what?" she asked.

"Well—" He hesitated, because the answer wasn't clear. How long would it take to remove the threat to her life?

"You'll have to leave it up to the BKA," he said. "I'm not sure how long they'll let me stay in Berlin."

"You plan to arrest this man?"

"We need him alive, yes."

She shook her head. "Kill him. For me. For Karina."

"I can't promise you, Iva."

"Can't or won't?"

Slayton clenched his jaw. He knew what she wanted. He wanted the same. But he'd promised to behave. The bigger picture was clear in his mind. And the room was probably bugged. Gerheardt and the tall blonde who never smiled were likely listening to every word he and Iva said.

"He'll pay for what he did. I can promise you that much," Slayton said.

"All right."

"I'll make sure you get out of here soon and get squared away with some clothes and things you need."

"Yes, please."

They watched each other for a few moments. Slayton had nothing else to say. He stood. She left her chair, too, and came forward to embrace him.

"Be careful," she said.

She squeezed him. He squeezed back. Slayton left the room with a grim set to his face.

* * *

"The phone trace cut off," Kara Botticker said, "but we did get a location before it happened."

"He figured things out and destroyed his phone."

"Yes," she said.

Kara drove, Slayton in the passenger seat. It was a little past noon, and they had to deal with heavy traffic, but still made good time to their destination. Slayton didn't know the bar she was taking them to, but Kara assured him she was familiar with the tavern and what went on in the back rooms. She'd told him the tavern's owner, Klaus, was a known suspect in the left-wing underground. He had ties to more groups than just the New Faction, she said. He hosted many such groups in the back rooms of his place of business.

"He'll try and get out of the city," Slayton said. "Or the country. We should skip the bar and try his apartment."

"I think you're right."

She changed lanes and made a left, a very fast left. Slayton appreciated how tight his seat belt held him in place. The car was a standard-issue BMW, gray, with a strong motor. Kara sped past other cars with concentrated skill. Slayton didn't interrupt her with chatter. At least they were cordial now. No more passive-aggressive sniping. He hoped they reached the same wavelength and bonded as a team. For now, he planned to follow her lead.

As she slowed upon entering a block of apartments, he finally said, "What's he drive?"

"Black Audi."

"That one?" Slayton pointed out the black four-door emerging from an underground garage.

"There he is," she said.

Slayton took out his CZ P-10C and checked the chamber. Loaded, ready to fire.

"If he sees us—"

"Looks like he did," she said and increased speed.

* * *

Frenz glanced at his rearview mirror. The BMW began closing fast. Eyes forward, he focused on the road. Cars lined either side of the street, but with long gaps between them. Midday, most of those who lived in the two-block apartment area were at their jobs. He had no other traffic to worry about at present—same reason. But as the road made a sharp turn to the left, the situation would change.

Frenz slowed for the turn. Ahead on the right, a large office complex covered nearly three blocks. Parking lot full. Frenz decided—

His scream filled the car.

He tried to speed out of the turn, but the BMW collided with him first. Metal crunched, glass shattered. Frenz braced as the Audi went into a spin. The car screeched across the opposing lane and headed for a light pole.

The impact slammed Frenz's head against his left window.

* * *

Slayton asked, "What's the plan?"

Kara steered along the empty street, gaining on the Audi. The office complex loomed large ahead. People. Traffic. He asked his question again. This time, she answered.

"Run him off the road."

"Um—"

"Steel reenforced bumper."

"Great plan." Slayton tightened his seat belt.

The Audi's brake lights flared as Frenz slowed for the left turn, but Kara pressed harder on the accelerator. The BMW surged with a grumble from the straight six. The front bumper smashed into the Audi's right rear fender. As Frenz was partly through the turn, the impact not only turned the back end into a crater, but broke the rear window and shoved the Audi into a spin. The Audi's tires screamed in protest at the violence of the spin.

The jolt to Slayton was minor thanks to his preparation and seat restraint, but it was still a jarring impact and rattled his body. Kara Botticker didn't seem to notice. Her slender hands remained on the wheel. She followed through on the left turn, aiming for the curbside on the right. She guided the BMW to a stop as the crunch of the Audi stopping hard against a light pole reached them.

"Move out!" Kara shouted as she unbuckled her seat belt and opened her door.

Slayton yelled, "Get down!"

The incoming salvo of automatic fire ripped into the BMW.

* * *

THE CRASH into the light pole slammed Frenz to the right. Reflex action flung him to the left, where he cracked his head against the window glass. The exploding airbags on the empty passenger side did nothing for him, except block his exit. He hurried to get out despite the intense pain and crooked vision. He moved by rote, practiced movements memorized and mentally simulated over a period of many years. He already had a handgun under his coat, but he needed heavier firepower to deal with the threat from the BMW. And then he needed the car itself because the Audi was of no further use. Despite the pain, Frenz still had his long-developed tactical plan in mind.

Before he opened his door, he unsnapped the latch on a built-in break-away panel below the armrest. Mounted inside was a Beretta PMX 9mm submachine gun, with its stock folded. The flip-up sights were flat, parallel to the barrel. He snapped the front and rear sights into the "up" position. Frenz opened the door and rolled out onto the pavement. He left the PMX stock folded and held the sub gun like a pistol.

The BMW parked on the curb twenty feet away. The driver was getting out. A blonde woman. His vision spun. His head throbbed. The blood on the side of his head leaked into his left ear.

Frenz rose to his knees and gripped the PMX in his right hand. A man in the car yelled. Frenz fired. The magazine in the Beretta sub gun held thirty rounds of 9mm Hi-Shok hollow-points. He fired half the magazine. The rounds cut into the BMW's skin, punched through the glass. The blonde woman dived back into the car. She and her companion were seeking cover on the sidewalk.

Frenz ceased fire. He grabbed the two spare magazines in the compartment and rose to full height.

But his legs wouldn't obey his commands. He wobbled and nearly lost his balance. He leaned on the Audi for support. Frenz reached the sidewalk and collapsed, dragging himself behind the car.

Half a magazine...

Frenz swapped the almost-empty mag in the PMX for another. He stuffed the other full spare and the half empty one in his left pants pocket.

Have to move!

Have to...

His vision began to fade.

* * *

"He's hurt!" Kara said. She looked over the hood as Frenz staggered. Slayton put a hand on her shoulder and pushed her below the top edge of the fender.

"He'll take your damn head off."

"I said, he's *hurt*."

"You did."

"Let's take him."

She bolted around the front of the BMW, clutching her issued SIG-Sauer P-229. Slayton didn't follow, but instead broke left, around the rear bumper. He had one word for Kara at the moment. *Reckless*. And he didn't like it.

They were both in the open as they crossed the street. Slayton knew where Frenz's bullets would go if he missed —into the office complex. And while Kara hadn't called for backup, somebody had to have heard the first burst and phoned the police. They had minutes. Maybe seconds to get Frenz secured and silence his submachine gun.

Frenz appeared over the roof of the Audi and swung his weapon at Slayton. Slayton fired first.

He missed.

* * *

A FLOOD of adrenaline snapped Frenz back to life. His vision still wasn't straight, but he gained his feet and swung the PMX over the roof of the car.

He saw the woman in his periphery, but she was a blur of arms and legs. The man was the easier target.

The man fired first, the flash from his pistol muzzle winking at Frenz. Frenz didn't know where the bullet went, but it didn't hit him. He squeezed the PMX's trigger and sprayed a burst in return. But the man was already bending to shoulder-roll onto the asphalt. The burst fired over him and stitched the hedgerow marking the border of the office complex.

Frenz pivoted to fire at the woman, but she'd run further down the street to hide behind a parked car. He turned toward the apartment building behind him, part of his complex. A concrete path led deeper into the property. He ran lopsided, but he ran. Return fire—two shots—smacked at his heels.

* * *

SLAYTON CURSED as he rolled across the pavement and put his feet under him once more. He still felt sore from the initial collision, and now his left shoulder hurt from the roll on the street. But it would have been worse if Frenz's burst had hit him. Better not complain, he decided. They still needed Frenz alive, and he was running away. Slayton ran to the wrecked Audi and braced his arms across the smashed hood. He gripped his gun in both hands and fired twice at Frenz. The rounds didn't hit.

"On your right!" Kara yelled. She dropped into a squat beside him.

"He's not as hurt as you thought."

"He's gotta be running on fumes."

"Come on."

This time, Slayton took the lead. Kara kept pace behind him. The path wasn't wide enough for them to run side-by-side. Which meant a shot from Frenz might go through Slayton and into Kara, and they'd both be out of luck.

Frenz slowed and tripped as he neared the T of the pathway. If he intended to go straight, he'd have to negotiate a long patch of bushes and overgrowth before falling over the edge of a concrete lip. The gap above the lip showed a garage. Slayton didn't think Frenz would achieve anything by dropping into the garage. There was nowhere to go in the concrete-walled space, unless he had another car on standby. Frenz's next move proved Slayton correct. The garage was not his plan.

Frenz cut right, crossing over a patch of green grass, but he tripped again and fell. Slayton slowed, favoring a cautious approach. Kara took her opportunity to pass, running hard, yelling in her native language for Frenz to surrender. Frenz did not surrender. He swung his sub gun back at her and started to fire. Slayton beat him to the trigger pull. The CZ 9mm in his two-hand grip popped twice, then a third time, as Kara let go with two rounds of her own. The five 9mm slugs smacked into Frenz, and his body jerked off balance. Slayton's last shot split open the top of the German gunman's head. By the time his body landed on the grass, Slayton knew two things. He'd kept the unspoken promise to Iva, out of instinct if nothing else, and there would be no interrogation. They'd have to find another way to get to the top of the New Red Army Faction.

18

At least the bed is soft, thought Petra Shaw.

It took a lot of work and concentration to have sex with Niklas Kragh. The forty-something Danish banker with the thick accent had the looks, the hair, and a decent body. He had an appeal, for sure. But all he did was thrust and grunt like a biped battering ram, and her insides were a castle wall. He leaned over her on hands and knees, her sweaty thighs clamped around his midsection. They'd left the lights on because he liked to look at her, but it made it tough to hide her contempt. She had to keep smiling, which made her feel like a clown having a psychotic episode.

God, hurry up!

Lately, he'd begun taking longer, twice going limp and expecting her to revive him. He blamed stress. He made up for it with expensive gifts. She had a reason to be there, though. Kragh wasn't the only one paying her to get on her back. The CIA was paying her, too. And much more than Kragh.

Kragh's problem "down there" began two weeks ago

after a phone call. Other such calls had happened since, and she waited for the next one, where Kragh had told her he and his "friend" would make a final decision on what to do about "a problem." He hadn't described the problem. But she knew—or at least had an idea, considering what her handler had asked her to find. In the meantime, she kept up her stream of dirty talk and endured the discomfort.

Why couldn't I have been a dentist?

The phone trilled from the pocket of Kragh's dinner jacket. He'd left the jacket over the back of the corner chair. It was a ringtone associated with whoever his "friend" was. He stopped, panting still. Sweat trickled from his neck into the thick hair on his chest. He pulled out. She didn't protest.

He climbed off the bed, still very much out of breath, and tried to settle down. The ringing stopped. He went to his jacket on the corner chair. By the time he retrieved the phone, the ringtone sounded again. The glow of the screen was bright despite the lights remaining on.

Petra stared at the ceiling. Sweat covered her body. It didn't glisten or look good in any way. She felt gross. Wet, sticky, smelly—she hated it. Over the years, she'd enjoyed some of her clients. She'd had more than one who made her want to volunteer instead of charging. Kragh? Ugh. But he had wanted to bring her to Monaco. A two-week holiday. She got to wear nice clothes and eat fancy food. At least the hotel room had a view of the ocean.

Petra remained on her back, in the tangle of sheets, and listened to Kragh's side of the conversation. He was still out of breath, but managed to talk.

"Jude. What have we decided?"

The caller's name meant nothing to her. As soon as she

found out the topic of conversation, she'd send word to her handler.

Kragh listened. While he listened, he went to the bathroom for a towel. He returned wiping his face.

"I agree," he said. "I've been thinking a lot about our previous conversations. The matter is becoming complicated. But what you're suggesting will have consequences."

Petra grinned, turned her head to show Kragh the grin, and crooked a finger at him. He mouthed "no" while shaking his head.

Gotta keep up appearances...

He continued, "I'm in Monaco with a lady friend. Yes, we can trust her. Let me know when you arrive, and we'll talk in person. But I agree. Despite whatever they may do to us, it's time. See you soon."

Kragh returned the cell to his jacket. He smiled at Petra and returned to the bed. "Where were we?"

She gave him the answer he wanted instead of what was truly on her mind.

* * *

JUDE GARVIN'S HAND SHOOK. He used his favorite Montblanc pen to write the final set of instructions for his secretary. The Swiss banker, like Niklas Kragh, worked a legitimate business at a major bank in Zurich. His private banking activities were much less legal and causing the shaking. The Americans had frozen his accounts, making it so he couldn't do any business with his shadier clients. They were growing wary of his excuses.

He left his desk for the outer office where his secretary, Fiona, occupied her desk. He handed her the list of tasks and explained what needed completion in his absence. If she noticed his hands and the less than confident voice he used while explaining, she didn't say so out loud. With the instructions delivered, he grabbed his briefcase and told her goodbye.

"See you in a few days."

Fiona only smiled and wished him a happy trip. He pulled the door shut behind him as he left the office.

Fiona finished typing a set of letters and emailed official clients. Then she took her cell phone from her purse. Dialing a number, she waited for the party at the other end to answer.

Fiona took a second paycheck as part of the New Red Army Faction. Her job was to report on Garvin's activities and lately she'd reported much more than usual. Garvin had been talking to Niklas Kragh. Based on what she overheard, it had taken time to put the pieces together. The Americans were putting the pressure on. They knew about the extracurricular activities of both men and wanted something. For Alexandra Ruhl, the development meant only one thing. They were trying another tactic to get to *her*. They had no other leads but to go after suspected money men, but it was an important link. Kragh and Garvin knew too much. Fiona's job? Make sure the New Faction stayed up to date on their movements.

Whatever the two had to discuss face-to-face, Alexandra Ruhl had to know. Operatives like Fiona were in place everywhere to keep the organization out of danger.

A man named Philip Bischoff answered Fiona's call. The chat did not last long. She relayed the pertinent details of the Berlin trip. She'd made the arrangements, after all. She knew his flight, where he was staying, and the restaurant where he and Kragh and a third guest had reservations. She told Bischoff everything. They'd never met, but he was another operative like her. He ran an auto shop. After the call, Fiona decided to go home early.

She wasn't worried about the tasks Garvin left for her. He wouldn't be coming home to see whether or not she'd completed any.

19

Philip Bischoff already lived in Berlin. He owned several car service stations in the city. His double life remained a guarded secret.

Bischoff shut himself in his cramped office to make another call after Fiona's. Through the big window beside the office door, he looked into the garage. Cars on lifts, his employees covered in oil and grease. None of it mattered at the moment. Alexandra Ruhl was in danger. Two men she trusted to do a critical job planned to betray her. Their conspiracy had to end. Before they threatened the cause.

He reached a woman named Gabriella Scholl. She was in charge of a three-person cell—her and two others. The trio kept up to date on prospective targets, sources of money, and other field matters. Right now, Bischoff needed them, and their deadly skills, to deal with the bankers. He and Gabriella talked for a short time. The mission was simple enough she needed no lengthy instructions. But she did have one question.

"How much blood do you want in public?"

"Don't go crazy," he told her. "These targets are priority one. Keep it efficient."

"Talk like that will *not* get me out of my panties, Philip."

Philip shook his head. Gabriella could never separate violence and sex. He only said, "Do not fail, Gabriella."

Bischoff ended the call. He opened the office door and let in the noises of his shop. He returned to his desk to get on with the day's work.

* * *

"No other way?"

Rolf Gergeardt asked the question in a quiet tone.

"No," Kara Botticker said.

She sat with her hands in her lap and her legs crossed, stoic as usual. She answered the boss's questions with curt replies and only as much detail as required.

Slayton admired her ability to tell the boss what he needed to hear without getting into an argument. Then again, Gerheardt wasn't trying to push her buttons, unlike *his* boss.

Slayton didn't sit. He paced behind her. His answers were sharper, his tone frustrated. To Kara, it was another day on the job. To Slayton, it was a colossal failure on top of several smaller failures that had dogged him since the start. Frenz had nothing on him, nothing they could turn into a lead. The BKA's experts were searching the car and poking through Frenz's personal effects—just in case. Slayton and Kara's on-scene search only turned up a tourist's suitcase. Frenz had divested himself of any incriminating evidence.

One dead thug was how Mason dismissed the incident

after Slayton's report. *All your effort so far and one dead thug. What will you do for an encore?*

Slayton ended the call wanting to punch Mason in the mouth. Wasn't the first time, not the last.

"Dammit, Jack," Gerheardt snapped. "Stop pacing. You're going to ruin my rug."

"It's a cheap rug."

"Still. *Stop*. Look at me. We're talking."

Slayton ceased pacing and faced Gerheardt. He stood behind Kara. She stole a glance over his shoulder at him. She did not give him a happy look. She didn't want him behind her. He stepped left to stay visible in her periphery. This seemed to satisfy her. She faced forward again.

Gerheardt said, "I suggest—"

His desk phone rang. He reached for the handset.

"Yes? All right, put him through."

Gerheardt tapped a button to activate the speaker and replaced the handset.

Nathan Mason's gruff voice came over the speaker.

"Rolf."

"Hello, Nathan. I have Mr. Slayton and Agent Botticker in my office."

"Good. We have a new lead, and maybe this one Jack won't blow away."

Slayton clenched his jaw and balled a fist and let out a slow breath. Gerheardt raised an eyebrow. Kara sat as if she hadn't noticed.

Mason continued. "We found two bankers we suspect launder money for extremist groups, which includes the New Faction. We have an asset planted with one of them. It's a honey trap job. We've applied some pressure to both men. Frozen assets, obvious surveillance. It appears they've cracked. They're going to meet in Berlin to discuss the situation, and we need them for questioning..."

* * *

Petra Shaw inhaled deeply and let it out as she examined herself in the mirror. Good. The cocktail dress didn't rip down the front. She wasn't getting paunchy. She needed to look like eye candy while still able to breathe, which required her stomach to move in and out. The dress looked like it was squeezing everything out the way one squeezed toothpaste. But she was used to the appearance. So many of her past clients demanded the look.

The hem was also shorter than she preferred, but Niklas liked her thighs. She hoped it didn't hike up when she sat and flash her crotch to one and all, legs crossed or not. Hazards of the job, she told herself.

Petra had a bad feeling about the dinner and didn't want to be without a weapon. But her small diamond-studded purse wasn't a place to hide a 9mm or even a flat .380 autoloader. She'd have to risk going without. There was nowhere to hide a gun under her outfit either. A garter holster was certainly out of the question.

The hotel salon did her hair earlier in the afternoon, not long after she and Niklas arrived in Berlin. Her blonde locks trailed down her back in flowing curls. While sitting in the stylist's chair, she examined her face in the mirror, and thought about the circumstances in which she now found herself.

Petra had been a $1000 an hour escort in New York City. Her status enabled her to tip off friends to the rich and powerful who made up her clientele. Her friends then broke into said clients' hotel rooms to help themselves to valuables. One night, two of her "friends" got caught. They squealed and landed the entire crew, Petra included, in police custody. She was looking at hard time when a gentleman from the government made her an offer she couldn't refuse.

Her get-out-of-jail card wasn't cheap. She'd traded her independent operation for a CIA pimp. They now owned her till further notice—or until she died in action. Petra did what they told. Her current orders were to stay close to Niklas Kragh and find out who his terrorist buddies were. The only bright spot to being in Berlin was the charade was coming to an end. Her handler became very excited about the meeting once she'd had a moment to call and report. But her bad feeling persisted.

Kragh hummed a tune in the other room. He was ready. He had been ready for thirty minutes, but it had taken her at least as long to do her makeup. Kragh humming meant he was in a good mood. It was one of the few times he'd been in a good mood since she became his favorite lay.

Did he expect the dinner with Garvin to turn his fortunes around?

Petra pressed her lips together and noted the uncertainty in her eyes and her jittery hands. The mirror concealed nothing.

It was a warm night. If he saw her shaking, she wouldn't be able to blame it on a chill.

"Are you ready?"

Niklas Kragh stuck his head through the bathroom doorway. He grinned. "Wow! You look amazing!"

She smiled at his reflection and did a turn. He clapped.

"We need to go, my dear. I don't want to be late."

Petra grabbed her purse from the counter. It matched her diamond earrings and necklace. "I'm starving," she said.

Niklas Kragh offered his arm. She slipped hers through. They left the hotel room. They were dining at a restaurant called The Falko. It was a short car ride away.

20

Jude Garvin finished tying his tie and turned from the mirror. He was alone. No bodyguards, secretary, girlfriend. He didn't need any of that. What he had instead was a gun. He collected the compact autoloader from the nightstand. It was a stainless-steel pistol, a Walther PPK in .32 ACP. He clipped a holster to his belt and covered the gun with the flap of his dinner jacket. A final check in the mirror. Everything looked right. He departed for The Falko.

He never went anywhere without the PPK, at least since the CIA put their claws into his business. After tonight, they'd back off. He hoped Kragh agreed to the plan to end the problem. He was aware of compromising clients, but his own neck mattered more.

He left the room and waited in front of the hotel while the valet retrieved his car.

The bright lights of The Falko greeted Garvin as he turned into the parking lot. He'd reserved the private dining room. Diners packed the place. Garvin saw them through the windows wrapping around the front and sides of the building. He wondered if Kragh had arrived ahead of him.

Exiting the car, he dropped to one knee, as if tying a shoe. He scanned the lot. Other customers came and went, their jovial dialogue filling the night. What he did not see was anybody loitering. No lone individuals waiting in cars. The Americans had been watching him back home. Had they not followed him to Berlin?

The maître d' greeted Garvin at the door and escorted him through the busy restaurant to the back dining rooms. They were behind a wall, blocked from the main dining area via glass. Of course, Garvin knew anybody could reserve one as he did. The Falko was not a place where you escaped with a check less than $400 US. The restaurant was named for Falko Lasker, the current golden boy of German cuisine. He was a celebrity chef who spent much of his time on TV and less of his time running his restaurants. But the owner's absence didn't affect the quality of the food or the desire for well-heeled diners to pay a lot of money for the privilege of saying they managed to score reservations.

The private dining room was quiet, and he found Kragh already seated. With a woman.

Garvin thanked the maître d', who departed and closed the door.

"Who is this?" Garvin gestured at Petra Shaw as if swiping away a fly.

Niklas Kragh stood. He beamed as he replied, "This is Petra. Petra, my dear, Jude Garvin, an old friend."

Garvin reached the table and regarded Petra with hostility.

"Our conversation was to be private, Niklas."

"She's all right, don't worry."

"I do worry," Garvin said. "Don't you realize—"

"She's not going—she's not one of *them*, Jude."

As she started to rise from her chair, Petra said, "I'll leave."

"No, Petra, please, stay," Kragh told her. He turned back to Garvin. "You will find her stimulating company, Jude, I promise."

"Does she know about our business?"

"Only what I've told her."

"Which is?"

"The basics."

Garvin sighed and pulled out the third chair and sat. He glanced once more at the woman, then turned his attention to Kragh. He'd forget she was there...unless she made a threatening move. He had the PPK to respond to such an event.

A knock at the door. Garvin moved his right hand to his hip. The door opened and their waiter entered, introducing himself as Lex. Garvin almost forgot he should be consulting the menu. Keeping his right hand on his leg, he used his left to open the menu to begin looking at the choices.

The table sat in the center of the room, which wasn't large. One might call it an "intimate" setting, but it sure was Old World. Mirrors and paintings on the wall, antique cabinets and low lighting. It felt like a time warp to the 1800s. But Garvin didn't notice. He tried to read the menu only to have trouble concentrating.

They ordered drinks and an appetizer. Garvin closed the menu.

Kragh frowned. "See nothing you like?"

"Business, Niklas. We came here for a reason."

"Then open the conversation. Please. This was your idea."

"The last couple of days—"

"Have been awful. They're everywhere."

"If we run, they'll only know we're guilty."

"Then we need to surrender," Kragh said.

Garvin glanced at Petra. She watched him with full attention. He didn't need to prove his worth by having younger women around. Couldn't Kragh have left her at the hotel?

"We need to go to the Americans," Garvin said, "and tell them what they want to know."

"Give them everything? Or do we dangle a carrot?"

"We hand them Andreas Ritter."

"Ruhl's top executioner?" Kragh blinked.

"They've been hunting him for years."

"He's been hiding. Do you know where? I don't."

"I know enough," Garvin said. "And I know now is the chance for them to take him. The woman he ran off with? They had a baby. A son. He's vulnerable. He won't fight if his family is close by."

"What about Alexandra Ruhl? We don't—"

A knock at the door again. The waiter reappeared with a tray of drinks and their appetizer. Petra Shaw sipped her martini and began picking at the appetizer, as did Kragh. Garvin touched neither his drink nor the food. Kragh thanked the waiter and asked for a few more minutes to decide on their entrees. The waiter departed.

"How do you suppose we contact the Americans?" Kragh asked.

"We go to the embassy."

Kragh laughed. "We'll never get beyond the gate."

"If we say *his* name, they will figure it out and let us talk to whoever represents the CIA."

"All right. I agree. But we go together."

"Of course."

"How do you propose we spend the rest of our lives?" Kragh asked. "Once they get Ritter, his network will never stop looking for us."

"We'll need protection." Garvin shrugged. "Worst case, new identities. But if the Americans dismantle the entire network, we can, perhaps, go back to our normal lives."

Petra Shaw spoke up.

"They won't let you," she said.

Garvin regarded her like a cockroach on the kitchen floor.

She continued. "Once they have you, they'll make you reveal every other nefarious character you've done business with. They'll make you report to them when those characters do anything of any kind."

"And how do you know, young lady?"

"I know things you don't," Petra said. "I'd rather not talk about it. But understand you're making a deal with the devil, and the devil always wins."

Garvin turned back to Kragh. The Dutch banker ate his portion of the appetizer without a care. Garvin finally picked up his glass and sipped his pure malt scotch.

Kragh noticed Garvin watching him, swallowed, and said, "She might be right, but what can we do?"

21

Petra Shaw watched Jude Garvin and expected him to pass out. The man was a ball of stress and anxiety. And she should have kept her mouth shut. He didn't seem to like women very much.

But she was in a position to help. Her job was to pick up anything she could in their terrorist financing efforts. They wanted to reach the Agency. All she had to do was introduce them to her handler. She'd help them and score points for herself at the same time. Get the devil off her back for a while.

Saying anything outright would blow her cover. What she needed was to make a phone call and tell her handler what was happening and let him take over. If they had any local field officers, they could scramble and be at the restaurant in a short amount of time. Petra scooted her chair back and told them she needed to powder her nose. Kragh stood as a gentleman should, but Garvin remained seated. She left the door of the private dining room open a little behind her.

* * *

JACK SLAYTON SAT in a car parked across the street from The Falko. He listened with growing frustration to Kragh and Garvin. He wanted to go in there and tell them, "Hi, I'm from the CIA. Let's talk about your problem. How did I know? Easy. I bugged the room!"

He and Kara visited The Falko when it opened in the afternoon. Using a story about forgetting his phone the night before, they checked the private dining rooms. He planted a listening device in each since he didn't know which one Kragh and Garvin would end up using. The bug wasn't under the table but behind one of the mirrors. When the bankers began their conversation, he had to flip switches to discover which dining room they were in, then he turned off the other bugs. Now he sat listening and wondering what to do. The simplest course was to advise Mason and Gerheardt, or let Kara take them into custody.

Why did spying have to be so complicated?

But at least they had the goods. A direct link to Andreas Ritter. The mention of Ritter's name perked Slayton up indeed.

But the Agency had to make a deal. Especially with Garvin, who appeared to know more than Kragh.

* * *

SEATED in the general dining area, two people kept watch on the activity in the private dining room. They watched Kragh, Garvin, and the woman. When the woman left the table, the man turned to his female companion and leaned close.

"Now?" asked Johann Wessely. He was a New Red Army Faction sharpshooter, an assassin skilled with guns and many other killing tools. He was thin, with dark eyes and hair, and wore clothes a size larger to hide the weapons he carried. Tonight, a Glock-18 machine pistol rode under his black dinner jacket. If anything set Johann apart from another male, it was his rat-like eyes. They were a predator's eyes. He'd never exist within polite company. He was the type condemned to the underworld, and he relished his role.

The woman across the table was Gabriella Scholl, the woman whom Philip Bischoff called for the night's mission. Her thick curly hair defined her the most. Her slacks and blouse fit her thick but muscled frame tightly. She'd picked the outfit for the maximum movement it allowed. She could run, jump, and shoot. Her lace-up shoes only added to the versatility. No covert operator expecting action wore anything but lace-up shoes. They didn't fall off when the running began.

"What do we do with the woman?" Gabriella asked.

Wessely grinned. "Our orders are to kill the men. Nothing more."

There was a gleam in Gabriella's eyes as she examined the blonde woman in the cocktail dress. "She knows what the other two are saying. We kill them, capture her, and make her tell us what Garvin and Kragh talked about."

"Our orders, Gabriella—"

"But she knows what they've discussed. She can tell us—"

"Gabby, darling, you only want another plaything to torture."

"What's wrong with that? Plus, she can tell us things."

"She's leaving the table," Johann pointed out.

"Must have to tinkle. You only rent your booze, you know, nobody gets to keep it."

"You've said so many times. Many, many times."

"You don't like my jokes?"

"It's time for a new one, Gabby."

"She sure has a beautiful body," Gabriella remarked. She watched Petra Shaw until she left the dining room. And left the door to the private room open a crack.

THE TWO BANKERS continued their conversation in the woman's absence. They became more animated, with Garvin looking angry and moving his hands a lot.

"He wasn't like that when the girl was there," Wessely said.

"Garvin thinks she's a threat," Gabriella said. "Kragh's whore."

"Why would be bring her?"

"He gets lonely."

"Is it time?"

Gabriella considered the question. She scanned the restaurant. Customers filled every table. The conversation and kitchen noise bounced off the walls. The walkway between the dining room and kitchen offered unimpeded movement. A straight line from to the private dining rooms to the rear exit. The third member of their team waited out back with the getaway car.

Gabriella could be the first into the room. The bankers were expecting a woman…

"Yes, it's time," she said.

She and Wessely scooted back their chairs.

* * *

"Our asset called. Get in there and make contact."

Slayton wasn't going to argue with Mason's order. It cut through the complications. Ending the call as he exited the car, Slayton waved at Kara. She waited in her own vehicle and rushed out to join him. They jogged toward The Falko's front door.

* * *

Gabriella took the lead. Wessely reached under his coat for the Glock-18 machine pistol. They were far enough from the main dining activity to be out of the way of any prying eyes.

Where was the girl?

Gabriella swung her head left and right. No sign of the babe in the cocktail dress. She pushed the door open and stepped into the room.

Kragh and Garvin stopped talking. Their voices reached a higher level, but the argument was white noise to Gabriella. It didn't matter. They looked at her as she entered. She smiled to keep them from getting nervous. Her body concealed Wessely who followed with the Glock-18 in his right hand.

Garvin's face changed first. Benign interest to concern

to fright. He yelled something to Kragh, scrambled out of his chair, and reached for his right hip.

Gabriella sidestepped. Wessely raised his machine pistol and squeezed off a burst. The Glock spat flame from the muzzle and the compensator cuts in the barrel. The front of Garvin's white shirt turned red as the 9mm slugs ripped through his chest. He choked out a scream as he fell and hit the floor hard. A handgun tumbled from his belt and onto the carpet.

Kragh screamed as Garvin died, but Gabriella didn't wait for Wessely to adjust his aim. She pulled up her blouse to go for the compact autoloader she carried appendix-style. She shot Kragh in the left eye, then moved around the table to fire twice more into his body after he fell.

She and Wessely had no need to communicate. They put away their guns in unison and turned to the door. Gabriella heard the commotion and screaming from the main section of the restaurant. But she had only one goal now. Escape.

22

Slayton and Kara dressed nicely enough to match the attire of The Falko's clientele. They bypassed the maître d' by saying they were meeting friends who had arrived before them. Halfway down the walkway to the private rooms, Kara grabbed Slayton's left arm. Her gasp was all the signal he needed to understand they were too late. The enemy beat them to the goal once more.

The windows of the private room barely muted the crackle of the Glock-18. The effect on the intended target wasn't in doubt. Jude Garvin, on his feet, went down with his white shirt stained red. A woman shot Kragh. Slayton did not see Petra Shaw anywhere.

Kara took over. This was her territory, and Slayton didn't get in the way.

"BKA!" she yelled, advancing, despite the screams and commotion commencing after the gunfire. They ran ahead, into the onrush of diners running for their lives.

Slayton didn't recognize the killers, but he knew a sharpshooter when he saw one. The man with the machine pistol knew his business. Kara yelled for them to stop and drop their weapons. Then she fired twice. The killers' rapid movement helped them avoid the shots. Slayton and Kara broke for cover as another burst from the Glock-18 split the air. This time, the blast was louder. This time, the panic spread faster.

Slayton glanced back. A woman was screaming, struggling to rise from where she fell, blood on her dress, a man trying to help her up. He faced forward and fired at the retreating pair as they moved to the rear.

"Come on!" Kara shouted. She ran ahead, Slayton following.

The killers made a left around a corner. Slayton heard another woman scream. The scream was closer, louder, and from the direction the killers had gone.

* * *

Gabriella finally found her opportunity to grab Kragh's girlfriend.

As they headed for the rear exit, the woman in blue emerged from the ladies' room around the corner. Gabriella grabbed her around the neck. The woman screamed, Gabriella pressing the muzzle of her pistol into the woman's neck. Wessely reloaded his weapon and ran for the back door. He held it open for Gabriella and the woman, then steadied his machine pistol down the hall. When he saw the interlopers advancing in their direction, he fired another burst. He didn't stay to see if he hit anything. He followed the women outside, let the door slam, and ran toward an approaching car. The headlights of the sedan bathed him in bright light. Their getaway driver hadn't fallen asleep at the crucial moment. He was on schedule to get them away from the murder scene.

* * *

THE GETAWAY DRIVER, Armin Gessner, yelled for Wessely to hurry. Wessely pulled the door shut as he piled inside. Gessner floored the pedal and screeched away. Wessely heard commotion from the back seat and turned to look.

The woman in the cocktail dress slapped and scratched Gabriella. She wedged a knee between them to kick Gabriella across the back seat and into the opposite door. Gabriella raised her pistol, but Kragh's date pressed her attack. She swung at Gabriella and knocked the gun out of her hand. The pistol sailed past Wessely's face to *thunk* into the dash. The woman in the cocktail dress twisted around to go for her door handle. Wessely got to his knees on his seat and smacked her in the head with the Glock. The woman went limp. Her head crunched into the panel below the window. She lay still, her dress askew. The hem ended up hiked over her rear end. The tiny string of her thong showed off the most toned female bottom Wessely had seen in a long time.

Gabriella hit him. Trance broken, he turned to her with stunned eyes.

"If you're done staring at her ass, hand me my gun."

Wessely laughed. "Your grip needs work. Back to Pakistan for you!"

"Get. My. *Gun.*"

Gessner, the driver, shouted, "Stop yelling!"

"Shut up and drive to the hideout!" Gabriella shouted back.

Gessner grumbled under his breath and steered through traffic. Wessely retrieved Gabriella's pistol from the floor, handed it to her, and sat forward. He fastened his seat belt.

"Give the girl some dignity, eh?" he told Gabriella.

But Gabriella scoffed and settled in her seat behind Gessner. "Bitch is lucky I don't tear the whole outfit off."

"Save it for later."

"Oh, we'll have a good time with this one, don't worry."

Gessner stayed quiet and drove.

* * *

Slayton dived for Kara and pinned her to the cold floor as the salvo of 9mm auto fire tore chunks out of the wall. When the shooting stopped, he took the lead, only to see the exit door slam. Who had screamed? Petra Shaw? He ran, Kara at his heels. He paused by the door, but Kara barreled through, bending low and cutting right.

"Crazy," Slayton muttered. But nobody opened fire. He ran out, cut left, and spotted the fleeing car with four people inside. Two women in the back struggled and fought. Kara took aim. He yelled for her not to shoot. She lowered her gun and started running for her car. All the way around front. Slayton watched the fleeing vehicle head for the street.

He ran after Kara and reached the government BMW as she started the motor. She drove for the exit, but then slammed the brakes. Two Berlin police cars bounced into the parking lot. One flashed past, but the other stopped to block them from going forward.

Kara shoved open her door and shouted she was BKA in

pursuit of escaping suspects. The carnage was in the restaurant, she told him. The cop approached and demanded her identification.

Slayton glanced right. A man hurrying to mount a motorcycle changed his mind and crossed toward them, trying to get the cop's attention. Slayton left the BMW and ran to the rider, grabbing the man's right arm. He held his keys in his right hand, and Slayton pried them from the man's grasp, dealing with the sudden resistance with a punch to the belly. The rider doubled over. He mounted the motorcycle, fired the engine to life, and shot past the police car. He turned right and raced in the direction of the enemy car.

The New Faction killers were easy to spot in the moderate traffic. The getaway driver weaved in and out of lanes, passing others at high speed. Slayton twisted the throttle and sped up to close the distance. He weaved around cars, too. The cold night air whipped at his face and stung his eyes, but he pressed forward. He needed Petra Shaw alive. He couldn't allow the enemy to win once more.

23

THERE WASN'T A LOT OF ROOM FOR RECKLESSNESS—FOR SLAYTON or the killers. They had to deal with two lanes and a center divider with colored concrete pylons. The enemy driver flashed lights and honked his horn to get other motorists out of the way. He slid through the gaps, changing lanes rapidly to get ahead. He sped through a wide intersection, then resumed the routine. Slayton stayed on the car's tail. They weren't going to shake him.

The motorcycle didn't require as much room as the enemy sedan. Slayton weaved through traffic with ease, and they cruised through another intersection. They couldn't get to their hideout—or whatever their destination—without shaking him loose or blowing him away.

Another problem. The cops were gaining fast.

Slayton watched in the rearview mirror. Drivers behind him pulled over to allow the lone police cruiser to use the entire roadway. Slayton sped up, dodging more cars, another intersection looming ahead. The light went from green to yellow to red. Slayton used the very narrow left shoulder to squeeze by, hoping he didn't strike one of the pylons passing within an inch or less. The enemy car sped through the light and turned left. Other drivers braked, honking. Tires screeched, metal crashed. Slayton steered around the collision. The New Faction killers made it through the sharp left turn onto another street.

The man on the passenger side, the one with the machine pistol, shoved his body half out of the car and aimed over the roof. Slayton zigzagged as bursts of 9mm slugs spit from the muzzle. Some of the rounds careened off the blacktop. As they straightened out of the turn, Slayton snatched his pistol from under his left arm. He aimed and fired. The gunman didn't fall, but he did fire back. The burst connected with the motorcycle.

The front tire popped and shredded under the spinning wheel. Slayton let go of his gun and tried to steer the motorcycle off the road, but no dice.

The bike spun out of control, and Slayton didn't want a hospital stay to make his mission any tougher. Engaging the throttle and throwing his weight to the rear, he released the handlebars and pushed with both legs, sliding off the seat. His feet hit the pavement, and he fell to the ground and tumbled. The motorcycle tipped over and scraped across the asphalt as it headed for a collision with a light pole.

Traffic stopped. Drivers stared. Police sirens wailed. Slayton stood and walked unsteadily to where his handgun had fallen. He had both hands in the air as the first police cruiser stopped in front of him. Two more followed. Their cherry lights flashed brightly. Slayton squinted against the glare. He wanted to argue the real bad guys were getting away, but knew the Berlin cops wouldn't listen. And he wondered how long they'd detain him.

* * *

SLAYTON DECLINED A MEDIC. Cuffed and stuffed into the back of a patrol car, he remained silent for the trip to the nearest police station. He'd skinned his knees and hands jumping off the bike, but the pain was minor enough to ignore. He remained silent at the station and officers shoved him into a holding cell. A bunch of other tough-looking misfits glared at him as he joined their pack.

How am I going to explain this? He found a spot on the long bench against the wall and settled down to wait.

Gerheardt wasn't going to be happy. Ditto Kara Botticker. And Slayton didn't want to *think* about Nathan Mason's reaction. Reema, however, might find amusement in his misfortune. Meanwhile, the enemy had escaped with a CIA asset who may have been their only hope for a lead to Andreas Ritter.

* * *

THEY TOOK HIS WATCH. Slayton had no idea how much time passed, but it seemed like it was forever until help arrived. When Kara Botticker stepped in front of the holding cell with a uniformed officer, she wasn't smiling. As usual. But this time, her frown communicated much more. She was mad. The officer didn't look happy either as he unlocked the cell and ordered him out.

Kara took charge of him and slammed a tote bag into his chest as they exited the building. Slayton grabbed at it before she let go.

"Your gear," she said.

"Thanks."

"I should have left you there. What were you thinking?"

"I was thinking I could move faster without you."

"Are you serious?"

"Partly. The other part was the conversation in the dining room. They mentioned Andreas Ritter. I've been after him a long time. He killed friends of mine."

"If this is a personal vendetta, you shouldn't be here. You're too close to the mission."

"I'm here until my boss says otherwise, Kara."

"Or mine."

"Touché."

She cussed at him, and they reached her car. He climbed in and checked the tote. His CZ P-10C, slightly scuffed, harness, spare ammo. Kara started the car and pulled out of the parking space.

"Despite your best effort," she said, "we got lucky. The shooter with the machine pistol lost his cell phone."

"Probably when I shot back."

"The phone contained an address we think could be their safe house."

She turned onto the street and drove fast.

"We going there now?" he asked.

"There's a tactical team also on the way. We'll join them. And Jack?"

"What?"

"This time, you stick with me."

"We need to get our asset back. Top priority."

"We need the terrorists alive."

"You know what I mean," he said.

"I have extra tools in the trunk."

"Good. Can this heap go any faster?"

She drove her foot into the accelerator.

By the time Petra started to wake up, she had no way to fight back. They had her hands tied wrist-to-wrist above her head, and they lifted her off the concrete floor of a cold garage. They hooked her to a support beam above her head. When the three let go, she dangled above the floor at least three feet. She gasped as full consciousness returned. Her feet were bare. She still had her dress on. Her head hurt from where the gun hit her. Two men, one woman. The faces hadn't changed.

They examined her like she was a monkey in a zoo. They wanted her to perform a trick in exchange for a treat.

The woman smiled and said, "I volunteer to interrogate this woman."

The men grinned. Petra made eye contact with the woman. The gleam in her eye was one Petra knew well. The woman was a sadist. The kind who liked to hurt others—and got off while doing so. The kind who looked for mates who enjoyed being hurt. Petra Shaw wasn't one of those.

The two men turned away. Petra stayed on the woman's face, defiant, silently issuing a challenge. The men grabbed metal folding chairs and laughed as they sat. They were the kind who liked to watch.

The woman smiled and crossed to a work table against

a wall. She grabbed a small knife. Petra didn't have to wonder if it was sharp. She knew the blade could cut through steel.

Petra felt the sweat on her body. Rapid pulse. She had one last thought before the torture began.

Who challenged whom...

24

GABRIELLA CHOSE A THIN EXACTO WITH A METAL GRIP. SHE LIKED to use it to slice fabric. Such as the dangling woman's fancy party dress. Gabriella examined her curves and the swell of her breasts and the creamy pale skin and enjoyed the tingle through her own body the gaze brought about.

This interrogation will be fun.

She stopped and looked up at the dangling woman.

"I'm Gabriella. What's your name?"

"Go to hell!"

A smile pulled at the corners of Gabriella's mouth. She suppressed the reaction. The look on the other woman's face was pure defiance. She wasn't going to crack easily.

"All right. Have it your way. You were present at a conversation tonight. I want to know what the two men with you talked about."

"They talked about football."

"Really?"

"You killed them before they said anything you'll want to know about."

"Are you sure?" Gabriella reached up to feel Petra's plump behind and ran her hand down the exposed portion of one leg. "Are you sure they only talked about football?"

"I don't know anything! I was only hired for the night!"

"For both of them?" Gabriella felt the front of Petra's dress, belly to pelvis. "How much will you charge me for a night with you?"

"You can't afford me."

"But I get a sample for free, don't I? After all, you're not going anywhere, are you?"

The exacto gleamed under the garage light.

* * *

PETRA GASPED AGAINST HER WILL, but it was hard to hold in the shock. If she harbored the idea Gabriella had anything but humiliation in mind, the thought vanished when the sharp edge of the exacto knife met her cocktail dress.

The only sound Petra heard was the snap of the fabric as the knife split the threads. Petra watched as Gabriella pulled the exacto upward, more fabric tearing.

"Shall I go faster or stop?"

Petra tried to breathe. Never one for any type of BDSM, the current state in which she found herself frightened her indeed. This wasn't a John. No safe word would make it stop. She was under the power of this female freak, and nobody was coming to save her.

"No answer means faster, then." To the two men, "See? She likes this!"

The two men grinned. Petra shot a glance at them. This was entertainment for the pair. *Typical. Men are disgusting.*

Gabriella resumed slicing. She cut a long slit up the

side, finally exposing Petra's undergarment. Gabriella grabbed the side of the silk underwear and sliced, then pulled. Petra felt the silk fall away. Gabriella sliced the dress some more and cut away the front. Petra was now exposed from the waist down. She shivered and bit her lower lip to hide another frightened reaction. Gabriella placed the edge of her X-Acto against her—

"Tell me what they discussed, or I'll make you bleed like never before."

Petra finally screamed.

* * *

"HEAR THAT?" Kara asked.

"We got 'em," Slayton said.

The enemy "safe" house sat at the end of a cul-de-sac at the top of a hill in a residential neighborhood. The TAC team set up a barricade at the bottom of the hill and evacuated the homes in the cul-de-sac. They now awaited the signal from Kara Botticker. She and Slayton approached the house, moving slow to keep the bottoms of their shoes from scraping the driveway pavement.

Ear against the garage door, Slayton heard a woman talking, threatening, and the frightened voice of the asset answering. He exchanged looks with Kara. They agreed without speaking. Now was the time. The only way in was to blast through. Kara waved in the TAC team. The heavily armed unit rushed up the sloping driveway, and the hell with staying quiet. At the front door, the team lead yelled, "Federal police!" and two more used a battering ram to knock down the front door. The door crashed inward and the team raced inside with submachine guns at the ready.

The garage had a side entrance. Slayton led Kara around the corner opposite the front door. They faced a fence. Slayton dropped to hands and knees, and Kara stepped on his back to swing over. Slayton followed, landing hard and feeling a sting in both feet as he dropped beside Kara. She waited at the side door to the garage, and fired two shots from her autoloader into the lock. Slayton kicked open the door. They stayed back a moment, then ran inside.

Slayton registered the scene fast. The asset, half naked, hanging from the beams. Two empty metal chairs. A woman near the asset. Shouting and a sudden burst of gunfire from inside the house indicated engagement with the missing men. Slayton didn't hesitate. He used the Mozambique drill—two shots to the chest, one to the head. Gore splattered on the asset's bare legs, but the woman with the exacto knife collapsed. And gunfire inside ceased too.

Slayton and Kara put away their guns and went to help Petra down. Kara said she had a coat in the trunk of her car. Slayton uttered his own words of reassurance, but they did little to remove the look of horror from the asset's face. She'd had a hell of a night, he decided.

* * *

THE FLASHING STROBE lights of police cars gave Petra a headache. Or maybe she'd have had the headache anyway, after what happened in the garage. She sat in the back of the BMW sedan, wrapped in a heavy coat, and the concealment was welcome. She leaned back and stared ahead, seeing nothing, letting her body shake as the shock wore off.

She'd expected to die in the garage, alone, but she hadn't been alone after all.

The woman and the man who'd rescued her finally returned to the car. They'd left her alone while consulting with some of the other cops at the scene. The blonde woman kneeled beside the car, while the male remained standing. Petra turned her head, but barely registered their presence. She needed a long shower and a bed. She'd feel human again in a few days. But she also knew she'd need to be coherent for a short time. They had questions. She hoped she had the answers. *You can do it, sweetie.*

"I'm Kara Botticker," the woman said. She showed Petra her BKA identification. "This is Jack Slayton. He's from the US."

Petra said, "You're from—"

"That's right," Slayton told her. "Sorry we didn't arrive sooner. My name's Jack."

"Petra," she said.

"You from New York City? I hear a little accent."

"Yes." She gave him a half smile. "I suppose all I lost was a dress. What's next?"

"We take you back to my office," Kara said, "then we'll get you a hotel or something so you can get some rest. You'll be okay to go home in a few days."

Petra scoffed. "Sure. All right. Who's driving?"

* * *

Alexandra Ruhl normally didn't stay out past three a.m., but they had reached a crisis point. She needed to act. Markus Frenz was dead. Kragh and Garvin were also dead, but Kragh's female companion lived. And three important operatives hadn't survived the night.

Her driver swung the black Mercedes in a short right turn, through the open doors of a large warehouse, and inside. The car stopped in the middle of an open area. Several men milled about the stacked crates and forklifts not far away. Alexandra made a rough count as she exited the car. Everybody was present. The group represented her field team leaders.

She didn't plan to be there very long and had two tasks. Issue emergency orders and make an example of someone who had failed. The back side of the warehouse faced the Spree River. Bright lights above lit the area. It was cold, especially with the side doors open. Alexandra was pleased to see no sign of the guards well-concealed outside. They were ready to alert those inside to any danger.

"We have an emergency," she told the gathered crew without preamble. "It's time to destroy any trace of your work. Operations are on hold until you hear from me only. Do not panic. I can already see it in your faces. You'll be fine as long as you trust me and do as I say. Where is Bischoff?"

A man to her left cracked, "You mean what's left of Bischoff?"

"Bring him out."

The man who'd spoken turned his head and let out a whistle. From a dark corner, where a stack of crates obscured the view, shoes squeaked on concrete, and two men grunted. The squeaking continued until two men, dragging the limp form of another between them, emerged into the light.

Alexandra folded her arms and approached. Philip Bischoff, his breathing short and face bloody, lips puffy, and more such injuries evident on the rest of his body, raised his head to try and look Alexandra in the eye.

"Philip. You failed, Philip. Your people failed. And died. We have no idea what Kragh's girlfriend may know because your people failed to get the information from her. It sounds like Gabriella was up to her usual pastime, which *wasted* valuable time. You never should have sent her."

Bischoff started to answer but never uttered a word. Alexandra ended his reply attempt by drawing a gun from under her jacket. It was an old FN 1903 autoloader chambered in .380 ACP. It had belonged to her late husband. She didn't often get her hands dirty, but this was a special case. It was example time. Bischoff never replied because she shot him in the head. Pieces of his skull and brain landed on the warehouse floor. She ordered the two men holding him to dump his body in the Spree.

* * *

Her driver, as usual, said nothing as he powered the Mercedes through the empty streets. Alexandra sat in the back and thought over the next step. She'd made an example in front of her men. Now she needed to give Germany an example. And a warning.

As light from streetlamps flashed into the car, she made her decision. She had to send a brutal response to the German authorities. The best option was to activate a sleeper cell and tell them to get to work. One bomb, then fade away, until she reassembled everyone for continued efforts.

She wanted blood. She wanted broken bodies in the streets. She wanted to show the BKA and the CIA they couldn't attack *her* without facing consequences.

25

Rolf Gerheardt was on the phone when Slayton entered the office. The German BKA boss paced behind his desk but gestured for Slayton to sit if he wanted. Slayton remained standing. He'd been sitting for the last few hours, and it felt good to stretch his legs.

Gerheardt remained quiet as he listened. Then, "He's here for an update now, Nathan. I'll get back to you." He hung up and raised an eyebrow at Slayton. "Your boss seems to know what happened before we do. Are you talking to him before me?"

"It's the way he is. We all wonder how he does it. Then again, he's a widower. Work is pretty much all he has, so he throws himself into it."

"Does that explain—"

"Some. Not all. He just gets cranky easily."

"You probably liked your old boss better."

"I say so often." Slayton smiled a little.

"All right, let's have the latest. What has she said?"

"Two names. One we know, one we don't. Or, at least, I

don't. She said Kragh and Garvin mentioned Andreas Ritter, whom I've been after a long time."

"He's one of their field commanders."

"And the man responsible for bombing a restaurant in California ten years ago. I was there. A bunch of my buddies died in the explosion."

"I'm sorry. The other name?"

"Alexandra Ruhl. Mystery to me. Mean anything to you?"

Gerheardt nodded. "Alexandra Ruhl runs a charity dedicated to ending world hunger. Inherited the program from her husband. Doesn't appear to be the terrorist type. Is your asset sure about the name?"

"I went back to my recording on the conversation to make sure Petra got it right. She is not mistaken. Could there be another person with the same name?"

"We can check. Sit down, I'm tired of standing."

Slayton took one of the chairs in front of the desk. Gerheardt consulted a page of notes on a spiral pad. "The house didn't reveal much," he said. "The bodies, though—"

"Who were they?"

Gerheardt ran down the three names.

"Known to your office?"

"No, and this is what bothers me. Our intel on the New Faction isn't as good as we thought. These names, these three individuals, are nowhere on our radar. It means there are many others we don't know about, too."

"And?"

"A fourth name—a murder victim—found in the Spree. Auto mechanic named Philip Bischoff. No record. No criminal ties. But somebody worked him over before they shot him. What are the odds he turns up in this condition on the same night? In fact, a few hours after the other three make their exit from this mortal coil."

"No coincidences."

"Yes. But it also means we're blind. How many more like him are there?"

"Time to blitz," Slayton said. "Round up all the suspects you have and make them talk."

"We can't *make* them do anything, Jack."

"You know what I mean."

"The informant who started all this, brought you here. The woman, Radler? Correct?"

"Correct."

"If she was going to reveal Alexandra Ruhl as the leader of the organization—"

"And she's the charity maven you say, it would have been a big deal."

"We need to tread carefully. Alexandra Ruhl has friends in high places."

"I may have an idea," Slayton said, "but I need some rest. Then we need to know where she is currently."

"Easy enough. What are we doing with your asset?"

"My people at the embassy are on their way. They'll question her further. She won't appreciate going through everything again, but for now it's her future."

"You and Kara get some sleep, and we'll get back on it. I have a feeling we're onto something with the Ruhl lead. And it's going to take a lot out of us."

* * *

Kara drove Slayton back to his hotel. CIA embassy staff collected Petra Shaw from BKA headquarters. She'd seemed to bounce back from her ordeal during their conversation, but Slayton didn't know how stout she was. She'd told them her background and how she wound up working for the CIA. She'd been through a situation or two in her day. Maybe having been hanged from a garage roof was another day at the office. Who knew? What he did know was he and Kara brought Petra back alive and had new leads because of her.

He and Kara didn't talk. They were both exhausted and especially tired of talking. Only when she pulled up at the hotel entrance did he say anything.

"Good work."

"You too."

"See you in a few hours."

Slayton flicked on the room's light and bolted the door. He could've called Mason, but screw it—he was beat. Mason was probably wired back home, ready to chew him out. Not tonight. Slayton showered, the hot water loosening the day's tension, then crashed into bed. Sleep wasn't only a luxury. It was critical to stay sharp for the mission. He was closing in on Andreas Ritter, the bastard responsible for the deaths of his SEAL brothers. Ten years. It still seemed like yesterday. The wounds remained raw. Hank Downing's face lingered in his mind. The face of his kid was there too, the one who loved baseball, number six on his baseball team. The boy deserved better than what he had to deal with as he grew older.

Soon, Ritter would be in his crosshairs, and Slayton would end this fight for good.

* * *

Peter Drewes said to the man in the passenger seat, “What if it’s not as crowded as we want?”

“Won’t matter,” replied Arno Konig. “The point is sending the message the boss lady wants the BKA to receive.”

Both were thin, well-muscled, and grim-looking young men. Arno Konig wore black-framed glasses. Peter Drewes wore his thick black hair close to his skull. They ceased the chit-chat as the Central Bus Station, Berlin (known as ZOB), appeared ahead. Then Drewes turned the car into the driveway and hooked left for the main building.

Across from the main building were the passenger platforms, covered by sections of roof support by thick circular posts.

“Which one?” Drewes asked.

“Far end. Three buses there.” *And a big enough crowd...*

The buses sat in parking slots at a slanted angle to the platforms. Three of the big transports waited with a large cluster of passengers lined up to board.

Drewes parked the car in front of the main building. The ticket counters and a large waiting area were inside. “Maybe inside is better?” he asked his partner.

Konig shook his head. “We stick to the plan. Pop the trunk.” He unstrapped his seat belt and exited the car. Drewes pressed the trunk release and watched his partner open the hatch and reach inside for a tote bag.

The action order from Alexandra Ruhl reached them the night before. The pair knew why she’d selected them. She knew they’d target the bus station. Blowing up a bunch of morning commuters was the “strike back” she wanted. Drewes picked out the bus station as a potential target thirty-six months earlier. He and Arno studied the location and its vulnerabilities, but as Arno Konig closed the lid of the trunk and began his walk to the passenger platforms, Drewes began to sweat and shake and feel his pulse increase. This wasn't a *what-if* anymore. They'd put the plan in motion, and there was no stopping now.

Drewes and Konig drilled the mission many times. They knew the placement of the security cameras and their blind spots. He'd parked the car in a blind spot. He wasn't worried about cameras catching his face.

He watched Konig reach the bus platform with the tote.

Not long now...

26

Arno Konig adjusted his glasses. He walked toward the passenger platform as nonchalantly as possible. Cloudy and chilly, Arno was glad he'd brought his gray jacket. It matched his earth-tone outfit. He'd selected the muted colors to confuse witnesses. They'd have nothing specific to point at later.

He stepped onto the concrete platform and under the shade of the supported roof. The circular columns were thick. A person as thin as Arno, or maybe a little heavier, could hide behind one and not be noticed. Ditto his tote bag. Unlike Drewes, he had no second thoughts. He didn't feel bad about killing civilians. He knew if enough of them died, the rest would rise up and demand the dismantling of the current system—exactly what the New Red Army Faction wanted. The people he approached meant nothing, they were cannon fodder for the cause. The men and woman, the single mother with her child, fodder, all of them. Means to an end.

Carrying a ticking time bomb was never easy. What if it

malfunctioned and went off early? Or malfunctioned and failed to detonate? But a timer *was* the most reliable way to detonate a bomb, and he knew the position of the count-down in his mind. He had two minutes. Two minutes to drop the tote and slip away. As a fourth large bus rumbled up the driveway and turned for the platform, Arno grinned. The bus would hide their escape, too, for a moment. A moment was all he and Drewes required.

* * *

Slayton either consciously or unconsciously muted his cell phone before getting into bed and slept well beyond his intended allotment. It might not have been a big deal if a bomb hadn't exploded at a bus station while he slept. Awaking to a series of heavy knocks at his hotel room door, he pulled it open. He held his left arm across the front of his bathrobe. Kara Botticker stood in the hall and didn't look happy.

"You *are* alive. Is your phone on?"

"Did something happen, or am I late for work?"

"Let me in, Jack."

He held the door open. When she passed and had her back to him, he tied his robe. Kara found the TV remote and turned on the wall-mounted big-screen. She found the local news and left the sound muted. From the footage on the screen, Slayton didn't need anybody to explain what happened.

The ZOB. He knew it well. Three buses, each with heavy damage, lay under the rubble of a fallen portion of a roof. Rubble, smoke, bodies, walking wounded, and emergency personnel. The on-screen reporter detailing the scene was well away, perhaps across the street.

"Bomb in a bag or something," Kara said. "We aren't sure yet."

"And?"

"The New Faction claimed responsibility to a TV station and sent a personal note to Rolf."

"Which said?"

"*Back off.*"

Slayton and Kara said nothing more. Their gazes remained on the television screen.

* * *

"SOMEBODY'S COMING."

The tall blonde spoke softly. She stood in the doorway of her husband's den. He sat in a corner chair reading a book. His wife didn't raise her voice so as not to wake their baby. But he heard the growing rumble of the approaching helicopter, too. The baby would wake up at any moment.

Andreas Ritter closed his book and stood.

"It's okay."

"But it's getting closer."

"I'm expecting them. We're not in danger."

"You didn't tell me."

"No, I didn't."

Anger flashed across her face. Pavlina Ritter left the doorway. Her angry walk echoed on the hallway's hardwood floor. Ritter cursed and dropped his book on the chair. The chopper noise now filled the house. The baby started crying. Andreas Ritter got mad. He grabbed a pistol from a desk drawer and went outside.

His freedom fighter days were over. He was out—retired. Living with his Czech wife and their new baby boy in the Swiss Alps. People in nearby villages and their distant neighbors, as nobody lived close, left them alone. Everybody left everybody else alone, unless they purposefully sought company. Andreas and Pavlina Ritter did not.

Ritter slammed the front door behind him. He stood on the porch, under the slanted overhang. The chopper touched down twenty yards away in the open field. The rotor blast generated a whirlwind of debris—dirt, pine needles, the bits and pieces of a wooded area. Ritter held his left arm in front of his face. When the pilot shut off the engine and the wind faded, he lowered his arm. He watched the chopper cabin. A woman opened the rear door and stepped onto the ground.

He'd ended his time with the New Red Army Faction. Not because he lost faith in the revolution, but because he found something else to fight for, too. His own family. Plus, after so many missions, killings, and bombings, he became target number one for western intelligence. Better to further embarrass them by hiding than remaining active with a bull's eye on his back. Nobody wanted to say so, but notoriety turned him into a liability, too. If CIA or MI6 thugs didn't catch him, a traitor from within might get ideas about ratting him out for the bounty money. The last time he checked, the bounty was up to two million US dollars. They wanted his head *badly*.

Which made him wonder why Alexandra Ruhl called for an urgent meeting and flew out to see him.

She walked toward him, and he watched her. She wore jeans, boots, and a heavy plaid shirt. It was cold in the Alps. Alexandra looked older than when they'd last spoken, too old for the actual years between then and now. But he understood. Leading a double, or even a triple life, took its toll on even the most dedicated true believer. She carried a brown leather zipper pouch. It wasn't bulky enough to contain a weapon. But she might have her husband's old FN 1903 under her shirt.

"Hello, Andreas," she said. She stopped a foot or two from the porch steps. "No need for the gun, Andreas."

"I have to be careful."

"This isn't a trap. I left my bodyguards in the chopper. You can see them watching us. We need to talk. I'm *only* here to talk."

"Why? Tell me the problem."

"You know the problem."

Ritter tucked the pistol behind his back and invited Alexandra onto the porch.

27

THEY SAT AT A SMALL TABLE-AND-CHAIR COMBO NEAR ONE OF THE front windows. Curtains blocked the view into the house.

Alexandra looked at the trees, the rolling hills, and listened to the birds. The mountains in the distance, with their sharp peaks, grabbed at the blue sky.

"You must love it here," she said.

"This fishing is good."

"There's a lake too?"

Ritter gestured absently over his shoulder. Then, "Let's get to the point, Alexandra."

"I hear a baby."

"Yes."

"Girl?"

"A boy. His name is Jacob."

"Are you happy?" Alexandra said.

"I was. Till you called."

"I don't mean to disturb the solitude or risk your life." She unzipped the leather pouch and removed several pictures. Eight-by-ten glossies, he noticed. "I need to explain what's been going on before I show you these..."

She told the story. She began with Karina Radler and the arrival of the CIA officer assigned to collect her—a man named Jack Slayton. She finished with the events at The Falko restaurant and the ZOB bombing and waited for his reaction.

"Are you sure Kragh and Garvin talked about me?"

"We can't rule it out. Andreas, Garvin handled *your* money. And if they said it in front of the hooker and she told the Americans..."

"They could trace me here."

"But if you hit them first?"

She handed him the photographs. He noted the baby had stopped crying as he took them from her. The man featured in each photo was silver-haired, older, trim, with a look of lengthy experience.

"Who is this man?" he asked.

"Nathan Mason, the man in charge of the CIA's mission against us. Kill him, and you'll set back their plans long enough for us to hide."

"Hmmm." Ritter placed the pictures on the table between them.

"I have more."

"Where did these pictures come from?"

"We had sources at the embassy. Past tense. They're dead now."

She handed him another set of photos. This time, a younger man. A tough brute. Somebody who knew how to fight.

"Is this Slayton?"

"It is."

Ritter examined another pair.

"Who is this woman?"

"Slayton's girlfriend. Reema Ashraf."

Ritter set the pictures on the table between them.

"No?" Alexandra said.

"I didn't say no."

"It's not the same fight as before," she said. "Now you need to fight to *protect* rather than destroy."

"I know what I have to protect."

"Andreas, don't you dare—"

"Turn? Betray you? Give me a break, Alexandra. Your husband and I were fighting the war long before you showed up."

"Then you'll do it?"

"What happens after?" he asked.

"You vanish. Again. Like before."

"It won't be like before."

"Your wife understood the first time. She'll understand now."

"No, she won't."

"Andreas—"

"How can I reach you? I need to think. I need time."

Alexandra sighed. "The usual channels, but you won't reach me quickly, nor will I be able to respond—"

"Send me a few soldiers for backup. Just in case."

"All right."

"Go. I'll let you know."

"Andreas—"

"This conversation is over, Alexandra." He fought the instinct to put his gun on the table. She didn't need the emphasis. And he knew better than to try and show off. She knew what he was capable of.

Alexandra rose from the chair. "Goodbye, Andreas."

He watched her climb back into the chopper and went inside the house as the engine began to whine. He hoped the baby didn't start crying again.

Now he had to face Pavlina.

* * *

"You said the killing was over."

"I meant it."

Ritter and Pavlina stood in the kitchen. He leaned against the counter near the sink. She sat at the kitchen table. The space between them was wider than he'd have liked, and all he wanted to do was close the gap.

But how?

"Why are you considering going to the US then? They'll spot you right away. I don't care how good your disguise or fake papers may be," she said.

"Pavlina."

"You can't *do this* to us."

Now he knew how. The answer was obvious.

"Never mind the Americans or Alexandra or any of them. They can't find us if they don't know where to look."

"We run?" she asked.

"What else? There won't be any more support from the organization. We have our nest egg, and for sure we can find work. We aren't helpless."

"We'll spend a lot on papers. New identities."

"Haven't we already? What's a little more?"

Pavlina's chair scraped the floor as she pushed back from the table. With a smile, she came to him, and they embraced. No more spaces between them. They'd decided, and as he hugged her back and felt the warmth of her body, he realized it had been the only option all along. The fighting was over. For good. Alexandra had run out the clock. No more plays to run—except to run into the shadows, where she might extend her days a little longer, but the enemy would catch up with her in time.

Meanwhile, he and Pavlina had plenty of time to put the war behind them forever.

But first, he needed a plan.

* * *

ANOTHER LATE NIGHT at CIA headquarters, but Nathan Mason and his staff were wide awake. They'd followed Alexandra Ruhl straight to Andreas Ritter. A surveillance team on the ground trailed her from Berlin. Satellite tracking from space covered her flight. In one of the viewing rooms in the basement of the HQ building, they watched her helicopter land at the cabin. The satellite camera angle looked down on the house. They couldn't see the person who met Alexandra on the porch. But the video shot from the ground crew, about a mile from the house, caught the figure of Andreas Ritter. The zoomed-in shot captured Ritter's face. Mason had no doubt of who he was looking at, and Reema Ashraf, beside him, agreed. When the helicopter departed the scene, the ground crew kept their camera on the house. Mason and Reema stepped into a corner to talk.

Mason said, "Score one for our side. We can use a drone to take out Ritter. Then it's only a matter of dealing with Ruhl."

"Won't work," Reema said.

"And why not?"

"The Swiss government will never approve a drone strike, and if we ask, they'll tie us up so long, Ritter will get away. And if you break the rules, the DCI and the president will have your ass."

"Do you have another suggestion?"

"Jack is only a couple of hours away in Berlin. Inserting a man is easier than dropping a bomb. Quick in and out. We use the ground team to get rid of the bodies, and nobody knows we were there."

Mason frowned. She had a point, but why send a man when a missile would take care of the problem? He considered the consequences of an unauthorized drone strike. The missile would blow up the house. A fire could spread. Emergency crews wouldn't arrive right away. They'd find pieces of the rocket and start yelling and screaming. Never mind telling the president. They'd tell the media. "The CIA is bombing random Swiss citizens," or some similar garbage.

But an assault by Jack, quick and efficient, made more sense when compared with the big picture. But any misfortune on Jack's end put them in the same tough spot. He'd have to make sure Jack understood the need for keeping Murphy's Law at bay.

"What do you think, Nathan?" Reema asked.

Mason nodded. "You're right. Let's go back to my office and tell Jack to get ready to jump out of a perfectly good airplane."

* * *

Slayton relished the jump, his pulse quickening at the prospect of confronting Ritter in a brutal one-on-one. There was no margin for error. He needed his head clear, his emotions locked down. This was his shot to settle the score for Coronado and the Shipwreck Bar, to deliver justice long denied.

He sat in the back of a loud single-engine plane, its high wings slicing through the night. Clad in black combat gear under his jumpsuit, Slayton carried a pack stuffed with weapons and essentials. The pilot, navigating by instruments alone, flew dark at 1500 feet to dodge radar. The landing zone was a grassy field a mile and a half from Ritter's hideout. He'd link with the ground team for the final trek. Barely twelve hours had passed since Alexandra Ruhl's visit and Mason's action order. Surveillance confirmed Ritter and his wife were still in place, oblivious to the noose tightening around them. Ritter had no clue what was coming.

28

Slayton touched down without incident. Repacking his parachute, he stashed the rig under a bush. He had instructions to wait at the landing zone and stayed concealed among the dense trees.

He used the time to press a com unit into his ear and activate the wireless pack on his utility belt. He'd be able to communicate with Mason at home base, but he was in no hurry to do so. He prepared his weapons next. He had a SIG-Sauer SG-550 rifle along with his CZ pistol, a knife, and a set of grenades and other accessories.

A dark-haired, sharp-jawed thirty-something arrived within thirty minutes. He spoke the appropriate contact phrase, and Slayton responded with his portion. The two men then hiked through the forest to the surveillance team's observation post. Two other field officers waited there. The post sat atop a rise, heavy brush and trees providing concealment. Ritter's house lay on a flat patch of ground about a mile away.

Slayton used his "Slayer" moniker for ID. The

surveillance team used their surnames. Ross, the one in charge, skinny and wiry, Templeton, the former Marine who met Slayton at the LZ, and Lorenzo, the quiet one who operated the camera focused on Ritter's cabin.

Ross opened with bad news.

"He has backup now." Ross spoke with a Southern drawl. "They arrived a couple of hours ago."

Ross handed Slayton a pair of binoculars. Slayton stayed on his belly and peered over the rise.

"What do you see?" Ross asked.

"Nice cabin, wrap-around porch, smoke from the chimney. There's an SUV parked out front."

"Three extra shooters arrived in the SUV. Ritter's vehicle is in the garage."

"It was only Ritter before?"

"And his wife and kid, yeah."

Slayton lowered the binoculars and turned to Ross with alarm. "Kid?"

"New baby, yeah."

Slayton cursed and returned his attention to the cabin. "They're all inside?"

"For now. I'd say they're preparing to run."

"See any weapons on Ritter or the wife?"

"Ritter had a handgun when the boss lady visited."

"He'll have more."

The cabin painted a picture of tranquility, but the picture was deceptive. Although, Slayton had to admit, it was probably plenty tranquil for the occupants when they weren't under surveillance. But he and his crew were also too far away. He wanted to get closer. He handed back the binoculars.

"I'm not interested in the wife or the child. Ritter's the

only target. If we can get close enough to take him out with my rifle, I'll call it good."

Ross said, "How close do you want to get?"

"The edge of the tree line looks to be about thirty yards from the cabin, right?"

Templeton spoke up. "It's twenty-five yards, actually."

"Better." The SIG rifle was good out to 400 yards, but to Slayton it was asking too much of the 5.56x45 NATO cartridge the rifle fired. And even then, it wasn't a perfect scenario. A proper sniper rifle would have been preferable, but they'd planned for an up-close hit. And nobody told him about the damn baby! Mason's little "hit and get" now had major complications.

Ross and his crew carried their own assault gear, foreign weapons with no US markings. Slayton would go in for the kill while they provided overwatch. Slayton departed for the edge of the tree line and followed a downward slope. The forest was thick but easy to navigate. He kept to a slow and cautious pace. The ground team was on his wireless channel, so they could talk if necessary. Slayton preferred radio silence for the time being. Ritter might have monitors listening for any radio chatter.

Slayton presently found the edge and stayed a few feet back. He found a spot to prop the rifle between two tree trunks. With the SG-550 set to semi-automatic, he wrapped his hand around the pistol grip, rested his index finger on the trigger guard, and waited.

A precision shot without a scope? Are you insane?

It wasn't an impossible shot, but he had zero room for error and too much on the line.

Ritter's cabin remained quiet, idyllic, and even non-threatening.

Until it wasn't.

* * *

Ross broke radio silence. "Garage door opening."

"I see it," Slayton told him.

A second SUV sat in the garage, black in color.

Ross added, "Ritter is in the garage loading suitcases into the vehicle."

Slayton concentrated his sights where directed. Ritter was moving too much. He placed suitcases in the SUV and went back inside. He didn't shut the back passenger door, so Slayton didn't have a clear shot.

Wait. Be patient.

The front door opened next. The three backup gunners exited. They spread out on the driveway, weapons at the ready. They carried short 9mm submachine guns. Weapons not designed for long range.

A woman in the garage caught his attention next. Tall, long hair tied back, wearing loose clothing. She held the baby. Ritter followed her, but the open door of the SUV was still in the way. She said something to him as she squeezed between the garage wall and the outer edge of the door. Ritter followed her and stood behind his wife holding the door as she put the baby inside. She leaned halfway into the SUV.

Ritter stood exposed. His attention was on his wife and child.

Slayton's gloved index finger tightened on the trigger.

The SIG rifle cracked once.

* * *

Slayton would admit later the presence of the baby threw off his focus and his original plan of a straightforward attack. Terrorists weren't supposed to have children. They were supposed to snarl and drool and hide under rocks and scream about revolution. But real life wasn't black and white.

The 5.56x45mm slug crossed the gap between Slayton and Ritter at 3,250 feet per second. The blink of an eye. But the bullet missed Ritter's head and smacked with authority into the door's window glass. The shattered shards showered both Ritter and his wife. Slayton gave Ritter credit, though. He jumped in front of his wife and yelled at the gunners. He needn't have bothered with the return fire order. The shooters covered their VIPs' retreat into the house with a volley of sub gun fire. They fired randomly while moving to cover of their own.

Slayton fired back, single shots, missing every time because he was pissed at himself. Now he'd have to get face-to-face. It had been foolish to try the long shot, but he wasn't in the habit of shooting babies. He watched Ritter continue to shield his wife and child as they retreated inside.

"We gotta get in there," said Ross.

One of the volleys from the house nicked a nearby tree.

"Nobody's going anywhere if we don't take out those troopers," Slayton said.

* * *

The three Faction gunners spread out. One, the team leader, sought cover and concealment on the front porch. The second stayed near their SUV in the driveway. The third found a tree offering cover from the sniper fire as well as a view of the back of the house.

Christoph, the team lead, yelled for his men to cease fire. The stuttering submachine guns stopped. Christoph reloaded and scanned the tree line ahead. There was no further movement he could discern. The sniper had moved. He'd want another angle for his next attempt. They had to get their VIP out and away.

He kept his eyes ahead and spoke into a handheld radio.

"Anything from the back?"

Ekkehard, the shooter by the tree, radioed back.

"Clear. No hostiles."

Christoph wanted a scoped rifle of his own. Something more powerful than the B&T 9mm sub gun he held.

Ritter's voice crackled over the radio. A baby cried in the background.

"Tell me what's happening!"

"All quiet. Stay inside for now."

Christoph still heard the baby crying through the wall.

* * *

RITTER RUSHED his wife and child into the house. The echo of the sniper shot still rang in his ears, but his screaming baby muted the memory.

"Spare room!" he yelled.

"I know!" Pavlina yelled back.

Ritter entered the spare room much calmer than he expected. A moment such as this was one he'd mentally prepared for, but hoped, deep down, he'd never need to face. The room had hardwood flooring and a square carpet. He pulled up the carpet and tossed it in a corner. His son was still crying, and his mother tried to soothe him. None of the broken glass had struck, so they knew he wasn't hurt, but the surprise, the noise—he wasn't calming down anytime soon. Ritter pulled on a metal handle and opened the first of two hinged panels. The panels revealed a shallow hiding spot under the floor. Pavlina stepped down without a word. She sat and held the baby close. Her pleading eyes said more than any words could communicate.

Ritter only had one answer.

"I'll do everything I can to keep them away from you," he told her. He closed the flaps and spread the carpet out again. What he wished for now was a soundproofed hiding spot. He still heard his son crying.

Ritter ran along the hall to the master bedroom and the big corner safe. There was no more shooting from outside, but he knew they weren't out of danger.

He spun the combo dial back and forth and wrenched open the heavy door. Various firearms waited inside. He wanted a long reach and a heavy caliber. He grabbed an HK417, a .308 battle rifle with plenty of punch. A chest harness of spare magazines fit around his torso like it was made for him. Ritter selected a BUL M-5 high-capacity 1911-type .45 pistol to back up the HK. Suitably armed, he headed for the living room.

He pulled a curtain aside to peek out. Christoph remained on the porch behind the thick wooden rail. He didn't see the other two Faction gunners. Still no shooting.

Dropping to a squat, Ritter flung open the door and belly-crawled to Christoph.

"Where are they?" he asked. Ritter scanned the tree line, but the density did not reveal any secrets.

"No idea. But somewhere."

"We have to go after them."

The comment didn't come from Ritter or Christoph. The words crackled over the handheld radio. Ekkehard, the man by the tree.

The third member of the Faction gunners, Wolf, added, "If we engage, Ritter will have time to escape."

"It's me they want," Ritter said. "If I can lead them away—"

Ritter looked at Christoph with a raised eyebrow.

"We'll engage and keep them away from your family," the Faction gunner said.

Ritter crawled back into the house. Christoph shouted for his men to rally. Ritter didn't look back. If they were about to die for the cause, he'd salute them later. If they killed the enemy, he'd celebrate with them...and his family. For now, he had to focus on drawing the fight away from Pavlina and his son. He knew the Americans. They wouldn't hurt his family. They might take them into custody, which meant they'd be safe, until Ritter found a way to get them back. There were plenty of options available.

Still gripping the HK417, Ritter returned to the garage. He tried to stay low. It wasn't possible not to expose himself. Christoph, Ekkehard, and Wolf let off a few bursts of auto fire. The gunners were running toward the trees, crossing the open space at a rapid pace. Ritter turned the key already in the SUV's ignition and the engine rumbled to life.

29

"Two incoming!"

"Where's the third?"

"Looks like he's staying behind!"

"Everybody spread out!" Slayton said.

Slayton and the three CIA men found cover, and Slayton told them to wait on his signal. The two gunners weren't approaching in a straight line. They'd moved out from the house in a sweeping right turn and penetrated the tree line.

Gunfire popped from the house, the stay-behind firing in a random pattern. Slayton made his body as flat as possible. Brush concealed him, but provided no protection from the incoming swarm. The rounds smacked into trees, snapped branches, whined off rocks—all near him, as if the gunner had a fix. Slayton figured he was only lucky. But if the bad guys had all the luck, he and the three CIA men would have to fight hard to make some of their own. The only reason to stage a frontal attack like this was to create a distraction. Andreas Ritter was making a run for it.

The shooting stopped. Slayton peeked without raising

his head. So much for a buffer. The other two Faction gunners were closing fast.

* * *

SLAYTON PARTED the brush ahead with the barrel of the SIG rifle and squeezed the trigger. His first shot was the signal to the others. But the Faction gunners noticed the brush moving and rolled to cover near them.

Slayton's burst went wide, the bullets chewing into a pine trunk. Christoph and Ekkehard reacted instantly. Their submachine guns spit fire in a deafening roar. Bark splintered, and dirt kicked up around Slayton as he pressed himself low. The sharp tang of cordite stung his nose. A familiar scent.

Ross, Lorenzo, and Templeton fanned out, each darting for cover—Ross behind a fallen log, Lorenzo behind a thick oak, and Templeton crouching in a shallow ditch. The CIA team returned fire, their rifles cracking in a disciplined cadence. They forced the Germans to duck behind a cluster of trees.

Bullets zipped through the forest, shredding leaves and snapping branches. Christoph leaned out, his B&T 9mm chattering. He sprayed a wild arc toward Lorenzo, who cursed and flattened himself against the oak. Wood chips rained down on him.

Ekkehard, more precise, aimed bursts at Templeton's ditch, pinning him down as dirt exploded around his position. Slayton seized the moment, popping up to fire. He caught Christoph's shoulder. Blood sprayed, and Christoph staggered but didn't fall.

Ross signaled to Lorenzo, who lobbed a smoke grenade. It hissed and billowed, cloaking the forest in a gray haze. The CIA team used the distraction, moving swiftly—Ross sprinting to a closer boulder, Templeton rolling to a new ditch, and Lorenzo edging toward a flanking position. The Germans fired through the smoke. Their rounds flew high, but the CIA team's response was surgical. Templeton's rifle barked. He caught Ekkehard in the chest as he peeked out, the Faction gunner's body jerking wildly before slumping against the tree, lifeless.

Christoph, roaring in defiance, broke cover for a desperate charge, spraying bullets. Ross and Lorenzo fired at the same time, their rounds tearing into him. Blood bloomed across Christoph's torso. He collapsed face-first on the forest floor, his weapon skidding away in the dirt.

The last gunner at the house fired, and the rounds cut close to Slayton. Ross triggered his response, and Slayton scrambled for fresh cover facing the house. He aimed for the retreating gunner and fired two single shots. Both missed. The gunner hid behind the SUV still in the driveway. Slayton adjusted his aim and fired again. This time, he scored, striking the last gunner in the back. The man fell flat behind the rear wheels with his legs sticking out behind the tires.

Slayton slapped a fresh mag into his rifle.

"Ritter's still inside," he said. "Lorenzo, Templeton. You two cover the back. Ross, with me."

Slayton and Ross broke through the tree line into the open ground. They kept up a zigzag pattern as they ran. Nobody from the house fired at them. Off to their left, angling for the rear of the cabin, Lorenzo and Templeton ran in a similar pattern. They also met no resistance. And then Ritter's SUV reversed out of the garage at high speed.

Slayton and Ross hit the grass and rolled. Ritter turned the SUV 180-degrees and came at Slayton with the pedal down and the engine howling. Slayton rolled some more, coming up on his feet to pivot and fire at the SUV's backside. He and Ross aimed for the tires. Ritter gouged the earth with his own zigzag pattern, and their shots only smacked the dirt. The growing dust cloud behind the SUV stung Slayton's eyes. Ross coughed.

Slayton ran for the remaining SUV in the driveway. Lorenzo and Templeton beat him there, and Templeton hopped behind the wheel. Slayton took the passenger side, while Ross and Lorenzo piled into the back. The key fob for the push-button start sat in a cup holder. The engine rumbled to life the moment Templeton pressed the button. As Templeton spun the wheel, a new voice intruded over their wireless com unit. Slayton heard Nathan Mason's gruff tones in his ear.

"What's happening, Slayer?"

"I'm a little busy right now!"

"Ross," Mason snapped instead. "Report."

Slayton grimaced but stayed focused on the fleeing Ritter. He was alone in the SUV. He'd left his wife and child behind. Slayton put them out of his mind. He had what he wanted. Ritter. Alone.

Templeton steered the SUV across the open patch of ground to the rutted dirt road. Ritter had a good lead and knew the landscape. Templeton faced a learning curve. And a cloud of dust which coated the windscreen and hung in the air in Ritter's wake. Templeton powered through and kept the SUV on the dirt road.

Ross finished his report, and Mason did something Slayton didn't expect. He rang off without another comment.

The SUV bounced. Slayton fought to stay in the seat. Ritter maintained his lead. He couldn't think about Mason right now. The mission mattered more than the Old Buzzard's intrusion.

* * *

RITTER NEVER THOUGHT the dirt road was so bumpy before. Now the SUV jolted and rocked over the unpaved, terrain and his speed wasn't helping.

He should have slashed the tires of the other SUV. Leaving in such haste was a mistake.

He couldn't shoot and drive at the same time, but he did have an ace up his sleeve.

A duffel bag full of grenades sat on the passenger seat, placed there earlier by Pavlina. She was always thinking, that girl. He wanted to smile, but she was back at the house, under the floor. In the dark. Alone with a screaming child. But at least he'd taken the threat to them away. She knew what to do next. They had a plan in place if they were ever separated, and a spot selected to run to for their eventual reunion.

And worst case...

Don't think about the worst case!

Ritter grabbed at the canvas bag and placed it on his lap. A switch opened the sunroof. Dust flowed into the cabin. He grabbed a grenade. He'd have to take both hands off the wheel to pull the pin. He did so. Holding the grenade tight with his right hand and steering with his left, he tossed the grenade out through the sunroof.

* * *

"GRENADE!"

Slayton knew one when he saw one. So did every other soldier. The grenade bounced off a tree. The bounce deflected it away from Slayton and his crew, but Templeton veered off the road anyway. He cut right, bumping out of the ruts, which put him on a path to smash into trees. The grenade went off with a crack and boom. Templeton swung back onto the road before colliding. He sped up. The rough ride worsened.

"I have grenades too," Slayton said. He reached for the sunroof switch. The panel in the roof slid back. Slayton didn't want to stick his head through for long less it be whacked by a low branch. But he could pop up long enough to let the grenade go.

"Keep him busy!" Slayton yelled.

Ross and Lorenzo, in the back, already had their windows down. They leaned out to fire single shots at Ritter's vehicle.

Slayton yanked the pin from the grenade, the metallic *ping* of the spoon snapping free sharp in his ears. He counted two seconds, grip steady, then surged up through the roof. He hurled the grenade overhand with a practiced flick. He aimed it to land ahead of Ritter's path, timing the fuse to burn short—long enough to avoid his own team trailing behind, but not so long Ritter could slip past before the blast.

The grenade arced over Ritter's SUV, exploding in a spray of dirt and rock that gouged a crater in the road. Ritter swerved off the path, his SUV clipping a tree with a screech. Shards of trim scattered into the underbrush. Templeton gunned his engine, closing the gap. Ritter wrestled his vehicle back onto the road. Their SUVs collided with a grinding crunch, the front bumper smashing into Ritter's right rear fender. The impact shoved Ritter's SUV sideways. His tires skidded until it sat perpendicular across the road. Ritter floored the gas, speeding into the trees, swinging the SUV left and right to avoid colliding with nature's obstacles. Templeton slammed the brakes. Wipers slashing through the windshield grime, then he accelerated again, pursuing Ritter through the haze.

Both SUVs started up a crooked slope, bumping over logs and tree roots. They bottomed out in the dips. Then the slope started down, and traction wasn't 100 percent. The floor of pine needles and leaves made both vehicles slip and slide. Ritter maintained the gap between them. Slayton lowered his window and stuck out his pistol. His first two shots didn't score, but the third did. One of Ritter's rear tires exploded under the impact of a 9mm slug, and it was game over. Ritter began to slide again, the slope steepened, and the SUV tipped. Templeton stopped and engaged the emergency brake. The CIA men piled out with their weapons.

Ritter's SUV landed on the driver's side with a crunch. It slid flat down the hill. A boulder sat in its way. With a crash, the vehicle stopped.

"Careful," Slayton said. He led the advance down the slope. The team spread out. Then they dived for cover as gunfire within Ritter's SUV cracked. Glass shattered. One, then another, grenade flew out the sky-facing passenger window. They arced toward Slayton and his men, and the blasts tore up more of the forest floor. Shrapnel smacked into trees. Slayton rose to fire at the exposed underside. Ritter came around the front and sprayed .308 slugs from his HK417. Then the terrorist ran out of sight.

Slayton broke cover and followed. Ross, Templeton, and Lorenzo caught up. Slayton paused at the SUV. He watched Ritter dodging obstacles as he ran and fired twice. Both shots missed.

“Where can he go?” Slayton asked Ross.

“There’s a road two miles away. A paved road.”

“He can hijack a car.”

“What do you want to do?”

“Follow me,” Slayton said. He took off in pursuit once more.

30

THE TRAPDOOR CREAKED AS PAVLINA RAISED THE PANELS, HER breath shallow in the stale air of the crawlspace. Her four-month-old son, Jacob, squirmed against her chest. His tiny fists clutched her shirt. The gunfire outside had faded and left an eerie silence behind. Andreas had drawn the CIA team away. Pavlina's heart pounded—she had to move, now, before they doubled back. She and Andreas had planned for a situation like this, and now it was time to put the plan in action. Andreas could take care of himself. She had to think about Jacob.

She climbed out, dust clinging to her sweatshirt, and went to the bedroom. She secured Jacob in a carrier slung across her chest. His weight pressed against her, warm and heavy. She found a pistol in the safe and tucked the weapon under her sweatshirt, the cold steel grazing her skin. She slipped out the back door. The hill loomed ahead, a steep, rocky climb through gnarled pines and loose shale. Five miles to the neighbors, five miles of hellish terrain. Jacob's wail pierced the quiet as she started up the slope, his cries sharp and relentless. Each scream clawed at her nerves, but she gritted her teeth and forced the noise to the edges of her mind. She didn't bother to try and calm him.

The hike was brutal. Thorns snagged her sweatpants, and her boots slipped on loose rocks. Each stumble jarred Jacob's wails into a higher pitch. Sweat stung her eyes as she pushed upward, her legs burning, the carrier straps digging into her shoulders. The canyon air was cold, but her body burned from the inside out. She glanced back once, but there was only the wind rustling the pines. She pressed on.

The neighbors' cabin finally came into view, a squat wooden structure nestled against the hill. The older couple, Philbert and Greta, stood on the porch, their faces pale, eyes wide with fear. The gunfight's echoes had carried through the canyon, and they looked at Pavlina like she was a ghost.

"Pavlina, what's happened?" Greta asked, her voice trembling as she ushered her inside. Philbert hovered behind, wringing his hands, his gaze darting to the baby carrier.

"Was that a gun fight?" the man asked.

Pavlina set Jacob's carrier on the sagging couch, his cries now a hoarse, hiccupping whimper.

"I'm sorry to bother you. We need help."

"Of course!" Greta said.

She motioned for Philbert and Greta to follow her to the kitchen, away from Jacob's noise. The couple exchanged a glance but complied, their steps hesitant. In the dim light of the kitchen, Pavlina's face was unreadable, her hand slipping under her sweatshirt. Before Greta could speak again, Pavlina drew the pistol and fired twice —clean shots, one to each chest. Philbert crumpled against the counter, knocking over a tin of flour. Greta collapsed without a sound, her eyes frozen in shock even in death.

Jacob's cries surged again from the living room, a piercing wail that cut through the silence. Pavlina stepped over the bodies, leaving faint prints in the spilled flour, and found the telephone on a side table. Her hands were steady as she dialed. First, her mother—three rings, then a hurried, whispered conversation. She hung up and dialed again, her jaw tight. She had to reach Alexandra Ruhl or somebody who knew how to locate the woman next. She needed to get to Zurich and her mother, as fast as possible. Then she could begin the next phase. Jacob's cries echoed behind her.

* * *

RITTER BROKE LEFT and started moving in a circle. Slayton fired at him, adjusting his aim with each shot, trying to anticipate Ritter's evasive moves. When Ritter dropped and rolled out of sight, Slayton stopped to reload.

Ross yelled his name. Slayton hit the dirt as two shots cracked overhead. Ross's return fire sent Ritter running in another direction. Slayton completed his roll and resumed the chase.

He moved at a slow pace and kept low. Brush crunched under his boots, but it did the same for Ritter and the others. The little sounds competed for attention.

Slayton crouched behind a boulder covered with moss. His pulse remained steady as he scanned for another opening. Ross, Lorenzo, and Templeton fanned out on either side.

"Ross," Slayton said, "flank left. Lorenzo, Templeton, cut right."

The team started to move, but then dropped into the brush once more. Ritter's rifle sounded once more, single shots whizzing past. Pines splintered. The forest was getting too dense to see Ritter's location, and Slayton doubted Ritter saw theirs. He was firing to buy time.

Lorenzo shouted, "Incoming!" A grenade bounced off a tree and flew another direction. The blast only tore up the foliage nearby.

"Move!" Slayton shouted. He sprang to his feet, his rifle aimed ahead.

The chase pushed further, the slope beginning to rise instead of continuing the downward trajectory. Rocks jutted from the earth, and the air grew cooler as the overhead canopy closed over them. Sunlight pierced the branches in golden shafts, illuminating the dust kicked up by the humans fighting in nature. The light warned Slayton of another grenade, as a wink off the metal drew his attention. It fell short and exploded near a stream. Slayton clenched his jaw. The smell of the blast stung his nose.

More stomping up the sloping terrain. When it started down again, according to Ross, they'd be thirty yards from the road. Slayton didn't want to hope for no motorists. He had to stop Ritter before he met the asphalt. If Ritter hijacked a car on the road, there'd be little chance of pursuit.

Slayton caught Ritter struggling a few yards ahead. He was slipping in the dirt as he tried to keep his speed up. Slayton put his rifle to his shoulder. Ritter whipped around, clawing a pistol from his belt and fired twice. Slayton didn't know where the shots went because they landed nowhere near him. Ritter's cold and defiant eyes met Slayton's for a moment. Slayton pulled the trigger. The shot was true and punched through Ritter's chest. He staggered and collapsed into the brush and slid down the slope.

Slayton hurried to the body, but found Ritter lying still, lifeless. There was no need for another shot. He was still looking at the grim sight as the other three CIA men found him.

Andreas Ritter was dead. Operation Iron Ghost was over. But the threat from Ritter's boss, Alexandra Ruhl, remained. Only a battle ended. The war wasn't finished.

"You all right?" Ross asked.

Slayton slung his rifle. "We need to check the cabin. *Now.*"

The team started back the way they'd come.

31

HUSBAND AND WIFE COVER?

If Reema knew yet withheld the information, she was laughing her ass off, Slayton decided.

He wasn't laughing, though.

One look at him and Kara Botticker trying to behave like a couple offered only one impression. Slayton was her hostage.

But Rolf Gerheardt insisted it was necessary to get them into the French Riviera. And back on Alexandra Ruhl's trail.

Ritter might have met his end in Switzerland, but his wife and baby slipped through—somehow. Slayton and his CIA team found the cabin empty upon their return. They had no idea how Pavlina and the baby escaped, though. There'd been no other vehicles. Had she run to a neighbor's home? And in which direction? Mason had ordered a withdrawal instead of a search. The shooting and fighting was bound to attract unwanted attention, and the Z Section boss didn't want his men caught in the law enforcement net.

Pavlina Ritter and the baby would show up again, somehow. Slayton was sure.

"Wives usually smile on their honeymoon," Slayton told Kara.

"I'm too busy looking fabulous," she said, and stuck out her chin.

Fabulous with a frown, for sure. But Slayton wasn't going to argue. The German federal agent indeed turned heads. Her yellow sundress was a perfect fit and showed off the right amount of toned and creamy white skin. Her long blonde hair and mirrored sunglasses created a striking alternative to the stiff law officer he'd come to know. She looked good, but vanished in the seat of rich and plastic around them, which suited Slayton fine. The last thing they needed was too much attention. And if being out of her normal work clothes made Kara feel fabulous, she might smile. Slayton decided he'd likely cure cancer first.

They were outside both US and German borders, and the BKA only had jurisdiction within Germany. The upper brass faced a few options. Make the mission a joint effort between the CIA and the German intelligence service, let the CIA handle it alone, while focusing the German effort on the charity, or a mix of both by seconding Kara Botticker to the CIA, temporarily, under Slayton's supervision. Both agencies decided it was more efficient to loan Kara to the CIA rather than assign another operative Slayton might actually get along with.

Problems cropped up before Slayton and Kara settled on the road to the Riviera—specifically, Saint-Tropez. They had confirmation of Alexandra Ruhl and her man, Frank Rosen, arriving. But the surveillance crew almost lost the pair along the way.

"Ruhl and Rosen made a pit stop in Vienna," Gerheardt explained, "and shook the watchers. Vanished. We lost them for six hours before picking up the trail again."

"Did your people find them because of skill, or did Alexandra want them to find her again?" Slayton asked.

"What do you mean?"

"They didn't stop in Vienna for mini-sausages, Rolf. She met somebody. In six hours, she could have met *several* somebodies. She's planned to retaliate for Ritter, and now she's setting herself up as a diversion to keep us occupied."

"Let's figure you're correct. Any idea of her target?"

"My people," Slayton said. "She had three CIA officers at the Berlin embassy working for her. Who knows what they leaked—but I have a guess."

Slayton called Reema and gave her the update.

"You and Mason will be the targets. She'll have a chance at me herself in Saint-Tropez."

"Will she send Pavlina Ritter?"

"She'll send somebody, and the odds are good Pavlina will want the job. How's your shooting eye?"

"Good as ever."

"You two get a couple of bodyguards. In fact, don't use company assets. We don't know how far Alexandra reached."

"What do you suggest?"

"Call Dylan. He'll help."

"All right."

"You nervous?"

"Are you?"

"If you only knew, sweetie."

Slayton arrived with Kara feeling 80 percent confident they had a handle on the situation. What he wondered was if he was wrong, and Alexandra had another plan altogether. Such as another attack on civilians. A civilian attack would be easier to organize and in character for her.

Alexandra hadn't struck at BKA in Berlin after Slayton killed Frenz.

She'd destroyed a crowded bus station.

* * *

PAVLINA RITTER SAT in a dim apartment in Zurich, her jaw tight. She clutched a phone, a photo of her infant son Jacob bright on the screen.

She'd left him with her mother. *Her* mother was all he had now.

Across the table, Peter Drewes and Arno Konig—bomb experts for the New Red Army Faction, the men who blew up the Central Bus Station—packed their gear, their faces grim. The charity front Alexandra Ruhl cultivated to perfection had collapsed under BKA raids. Accounts frozen, its workers facing tough questions from investigators. Yet Pavlina was going to finish what her husband had not been able to complete. *Kill Jack Slayton. Kill Reema Ashraf. Kill Nathan Mason.* The three CIA officers were responsible for her shattered life. They'd pay.

She'd argued with Andreas about ending the killing. With their baby now in the world, she didn't want either of them fighting anymore.

But the Americans changed the situation. Now, she wanted vengeance of her own. She'd been silly to think she could ever leave the fighting behind.

If the charity was of no use in getting them to the US, Pavlina had other means. She dialed an old comrade, Klaus

Meier, a former Stasi forger hiding behind a Kreuzberg print shop. The arrangements didn't take long. Several hours later, in a crowded beer hall, Klaus slid her three passports. Pavlina became "Sylvia Vossoo," Swiss-German consultant, Peter, "Michael Hale," Austrian engineer, and Arno, "Stephen Brandt," German IT specialist. The documents gleamed with a professional touch, but not an obvious one.

"Fifteen thousand euros," Klaus muttered. Pavlina handed over a wad of cash.

A night train carried them to the airport. Pavlina's heart pounded as they boarded a flight to JFK, tickets booked through a Vienna proxy. Pavlina, as Sylvia, sat alone in row 22, flipping through a magazine. Peter and Arno sat elsewhere, posing as strangers. No weapons—those waited in the States, via dead drops.

JFK's arrivals terminal buzzed. Pavlina stepped into the non-citizen line, her alias's passport smooth in her hand. The CBP officer scanned it, eyes narrowing. "Purpose of visit, Ms. Vosso?"

Pavlina smiled, her voice calm.

"Consulting meeting in Manhattan." The biometric reader beeped green, She was through. Peter followed, his Austrian accent selling "Michael Hale," though he stumbled on his fake employer's name. He attributed it to his bad English. Arno, as Stephen, glided past with IT jargon. They regrouped at a Starbucks. Pavlina spotted a family, a crying baby, and her chest tightened. Jacob's face flashed in her mind, but she gritted her teeth.

No hotels—too risky. A shuttle dropped them at a grimy car rental lot in Queens where cash talked. Pavlina handled the transaction, paying for a nondescript gray Toyota

Camry. They disabled the in-dash GPS, opting for burner phones and paper maps.

They hit I-95 South by noon, driving in shifts. Pavlina took the wheel first. By evening, they veered off the interstate onto back roads into Alexandria, Virginia, and checked into a seedy motel. Pavlina insisted on separate rooms, but didn't like being alone. She stared at the peeling wallpaper. *Andreas. Jacob.* They were ghosts now. And she was a weapon aimed at a target. Nothing else mattered except hitting the bull's eye.

32

SAINT-TROPEZ WAS THE PERFECT SPOT FOR ALEXANDRA AND Rosen, Slayton thought. You had a sleepy Provençal village combined with a hedonistic hot spot. The Vieux Port was a mix of commercial fishing boats and the superyachts of the filthy rich. Italy and Barcelona were a hop away. Algiers gleamed in the distance across the Tyrrhenian Sea. The criminal element remained undercover, deep in the shadowy alleys along the coast. While setting her trap for Slayton, she had plenty of options to also arrange her escape. New papers. Even an altered face. If they lost her in Saint-Tropez, they might never find her again.

But no pressure, Slayton told himself.

He and Kara checked in at the Hotel Byblos where high-rollers stayed for luxury turned up to eleven. A short walk would bring them to Place de Lices, the social center of town. Cafés, boutiques, nightlife. Vieux Port was less than five minutes away. The hotel offered privacy with its rooms and suites spread across low-rise buildings. It resembled a small village. Slayton and Kara booked the Missoni Suite, which opened onto a private terrace with a Jacuzzi.

Slayton eyed the still water in the Jacuzzi with a frown.

"What is it?" Kara asked behind him. She'd spread her suitcases on the bed to unpack.

"Looking at the hot tub," he said.

"We will not be using the hot tub."

"I'm thinking about somebody I could use the hot tub with," he said.

"Woman back home?"

"Who else?"

"Then you very well can return someday and bring her and use the hot tub until you both resemble raisins."

"I couldn't possibly afford it, Kara."

"You should stop being poor."

Slayton did a double-take. He had no reply.

Sleeping arrangements were simple. Kara got the bed, Slayton got the couch. Kara said if she was feeling generous, she'd give him the blanket under the down comforter. Otherwise, he could use one of the big bath towels for a blanket. Slayton took a deep breath and held his tongue. He'd slept under worse conditions. But with a friend like Kara, he wasn't sure he needed enemies.

* * *

Slayton and Kara went to dinner at one of the restaurants overlooking Vieux Port. The restaurant pointed to where the expensive yachts docked. Nobody wanted to see the rust bucket fishing vessels at the other end. Nobody wanted to view the local poor people, for heaven's sake.

Their table offered a view of one particular superyacht.

It was a sleek 130-footer with a cleaning crew working on the deck and along either side of the hull. They looked like ants swarming over a pile of sugar.

"What I want to know," Slayton said, "is how Rosen and Alexandra passed the customs check without tripping the alert."

Keeping up the newlywed routine, they sat beside each other, leaning close to hide their conversation. Slayton spotted a few American celebrities nearby, on holiday and bigging it up with the food and booze. Most of the clientele was not recognizable, but rich enough to afford whatever they wanted.

"If customs received the alert in time," Kara said.

"Or they're known here. Less scrutiny to familiar faces. But still. Even if they got the alert late, they'd have to know their so-called friendly faces weren't any longer."

"Which means a payoff, probably."

"Uh-huh."

"We have the boat," Kara said, "and then the rental property on the coast. What more do we need? They aren't hiding."

"Which means my theory is correct. This is a diversion."

The waiter interrupted them. Slayton's expression remained neutral as the young man asked if they were ready to order. If he noticed they'd barely touched their drinks and only picked at the appetizer, he didn't say. Kara turned her head to Slayton. She said something in German. She was acting as if she understood nothing but her native language. Slayton found it annoying. He kept his smile and ordered for himself and his "vocabularily challenged" bride. The line earned him the perfect scowl from the German woman once the waiter departed.

"That isn't a word," she said.

"What isn't?"

"Vocabularily."

"If you aren't more careful next time, he's going to figure out you understand other languages just fine."

"Are you going to be serious at all?"

"Are you going to lighten the hell up?"

Kara Botticker exhaled with exasperation.

"Back to business," she suggested. "What do you want to do? We have the two targets."

Alexandra and Frank Rosen arrived on the big fancy yacht, but weren't staying aboard. Their coastal villa had access to a private beach and several No Trespassing signs. A short wall surrounded the property. Slayton and Kara hadn't taken a closer look yet.

He said, "We can raid the villa, but I don't want to turn this place into a war zone if we can help it."

"We follow them, stir things up?"

"Stay aggressive but careful too."

"Does she know your face?"

"More than likely."

"But she doesn't know me," Kara said.

"No, she doesn't."

Slayton watched the yacht some more.

THE PARTY at Les Caves de Roy didn't start until one a.m. Alexandra Ruhl wanted to be there. Frank Rosen was her less-than-happy escort. They'd yet to resolve the argument begun at the start of their journey. And Alexandra had no interest in budging.

They sat in a corner booth in the back of the club. The low light cast shadows on their faces. The DJ music, and the crowd on the dance floor, covered their conversation.

Alexandra said, "There is no other way. We've set in action a motion the Americans won't forget. I must change my face if I'm going to keep fighting after."

"My point," Rosen said, "is you can't simply change your face. That's movie and TV garbage. You can't get an entirely new face with plastic surgery."

"I can change enough."

"They'll locate you again."

"What's your real objection, Frank?"

"I like your face."

She smiled and touched his hand. The smile turned into a warm look. "The new one will be nice, too."

"The doctor is going to tell you the same thing. We're better off disappearing somewhere."

"Like Ritter did?"

"Exactly."

"Where do you want to go, Frank?"

"I don't know. We'll find a place."

"And your other objection?"

"What?"

"Tell me what you're afraid to say, Frank."

"Well—"

"I know you too well."

Rosen sighed. "You're changing your face to hide. But you haven't said what happens to *us*."

Another smile, a sadder one, crossed Alexandra's face. Rosen stiffened.

"You don't mean—"

"Of course not," she said. "But it does mean the end. Of us. For a while. I don't want them to find me through you."

Rosen's mouth moved but nothing came out.

Alexandra smiled brightly, but the smile didn't change her eyes. She stood and grabbed his hand.

"Let's go dance."

Frank Rosen frowned at her. She beckoned him forward. She wore a yellow strapless dress and knew he'd find it impossible to refuse her. She felt like she was about to die, and if she was on borrowed time, she wanted to *live* a little longer. Rosen finally slid out of the booth and took her hand and led her to the dance floor.

33

ALEXANDRA'S STOP IN VIENNA LASTED SIX HOURS. SHE AND ROSEN completed their business well within the period.

They first visited the two bombers who blew up the bus station in Berlin, Peter Drewes and Arno Konig. She wanted them to link up with Pavlina Ritter in Zurich. She wanted them to go with Pavlina to the United States. Kill the CIA people responsible for murdering their comrades and disrupting their operations. Drewes and Konig had raced to a safe house in Vienna after the bus station bombing, but Alexandra found them less than eager to see her. Word of Ritter's murder spread fast, as did the attitude that Alexandra's visit led the Americans to him.

Alexandra was aware of the chatter. She understood what her people meant and how they felt. She countered with a different point of view, though. Had Ritter and Pavlina departed right away, the Americans would have found an empty cabin. Ritter's death was *his* fault, she maintained, not hers. It was enough to stop the argument.

Alexandra let her tone and expression show she'd not tolerate further insubordination.

She gave Drewes and Konig pictures of the Americans to hand over to Pavlina. They were to follow her instructions for getting into the US. Pavlina had contacts of her own, from *her* days as a freedom fighter, who weren't under scrutiny.

The next stop for her and Frank involved arranging for a plastic surgeon to meet her in Saint-Tropez. Completing their tasks, she and Frank spent the remainder of the six hours together. She said it might be the last time they had any privacy.

* * *

NATHAN MASON SAT behind his desk staring into space. His work, for the day, had reached a natural conclusion. A normal person would prepare to go home. He could continue with his various tasks and projects, but some of the work required the input of others. Those people had either gone home or worked on the other side of the world. He was at the mercy of the time zones and the time clock.

He didn't want to go home. His only companion at the house was his late wife's cat. He and the feline tolerated each other through mutual indifference.

Returning to an empty house was a tougher challenge than anything Mason had encountered during his CIA career. Leslie had been gone for almost three years, and he still wasn't used to being alone.

Reema tapped a knuckle on the glass door. He snapped from his trance and waved her inside. She opened the door halfway. She held her purse and briefcase and wore a coat over her suit.

"I'm going home," she announced. "You all right?"

"You ask me the same question several times a week, Reema."

"I ask for a reason, Nate."

"Why?"

"You often look like hell."

He smiled, but his eyes remained sad. "Enjoy your evening."

"See you in the morning if the world doesn't blow up."

"Good night, Reema."

She departed. The glass door whispered shut. He watched her walk out of sight. His gaze turned to the busy bullpen. The night shift had transitioned from day, and there was no room for him to get involved. He'd only irk the night-shift managers. With a sigh, he gathered his stuff, threw on a coat, and waved across the room at one of the night supervisors on his way out.

Heavy traffic delayed his travel home, and he took longer because of a stop for a takeout dinner. Chinese, his favorite. The stop-and-go and dinner pick-up served another purpose. It allowed him to check his backside and see if he had a tail. Reema told him of her conversation with Jack regarding a possible hit on him and her. While it made sense, Mason wasn't sure of the logistics. Could the New Red Army Faction get a gun crew into the US? He wasn't sure. But when the Faction succeeded in recruiting *three* CIA embassy officers, and there'd been no clue...

Mason hadn't survived the spy game by being stupid, so he had a pistol stashed in the center console compartment.

Not the best place to hide a gun, nor the easiest to access in a hurry. But he had the means to defend himself should the need arise.

And when Mason arrived home, he brought the pistol inside with his dinner.

* * *

On the couch, still wearing his shirt and tie, Mason opened the containers of Chinese food and watched a sports report while he ate with a fork. He didn't bother taking the food out of the white boxes. There was no need. His late wife's cat perched on the back of a corner chair, indifferent. A framed photo of Leslie was on top of the mantel below the wall-mounted big-screen television. She was still part of the space. He felt she was still there. Had she been, she'd insist he eat at the table like a proper gentleman. But Mason didn't see a reason to do so. He lived alone now, and convenience mattered more than "proper" eating habits. The house remained clean and spotless, though. Some habits die hard. There were some patterns he refused to break.

Presently the cat left the corner chair and curled up on the opposite end of the couch. Mason looked at the cat—Yukon, his wife had named him because he looked like a big fluffy tiger. It had made sense to her, and Mason was smart enough not to argue. The cat looked at him and yawned. They were both old, getting older, slower, not what they once were. Only Leslie had escaped the natural decline. She'd be young forever. He wondered which of them would join her first.

* * *

A PAIR of steely eyes watched Mason's house from the end of the street.

Peter Drewes noted Mason's arrive time. He was half an hour later than usual, but the takeaway bag explained why. Mason's pattern hadn't changed over the last three days. Home, work, home. No stop at the bar. No meet-up with friends. Lights out at eleven p.m. sharp. It was the kind of pattern a man followed into his grave.

Drewes's cell rang, and he answered. Only Pavlina and Arno Konig had his number. He glanced at the caller ID. Konig.

"Yes?"

"Is Mason home?"

"Where else?"

"The woman is home, too."

"Mine stopped for dinner."

"Mine didn't stop," Konig said, "but she took an alternate route."

"Good girl. Mine doesn't deviate."

"How much longer do we watch them?"

Drewes considered the question. Had it been up to him, they'd have hit already. But they were at the mercy of Pavlina Ritter's orders.

"Only Pavlina knows," Drewes finally said.

"Switch targets tomorrow?"

"Yes," Drewes said. "See you at the motel."

"I have some other ideas we can go over."

"If Pavlina's interested. I'm not exactly happy with how she shuts herself in her room."

"We can try."

Drewes ended the call and started the car. He drove away without headlights until he passed a stop sign at the far end of the street.

34

Reema brought work home with her. She left the TV off in the background and sat on a stool at the kitchen counter. The toaster oven filled the silence, lasagna reheating behind the glass. She'd made the lasagna last three days so far. If Jack had been home, it would have been gone the first night.

They no longer lived in Jack's small apartment. She wanted to live in something larger than a jail cell, so they'd pooled resources and purchased a condo. A *ground* floor unit with ease of exit in front and back—their only requirement. A fence closed off the small back patio, but Jack rigged a set of steps to allow them to vault over the top. But it was a long drop on the other side. Reema hoped a front door exit would be available in case of emergency. But she practiced going out the back anyway.

Lights above diminished the glow of her laptop screen. The data displayed remained free of glare. Reema didn't want the TV or any music on. She needed quiet to concentrate. She was still digging into the background and business activity of Frank Rosen. He'd been close with Alexandra Ruhl's late husband. Reema wondered if their romantic liaison began before or *after* Mr. Ruhl's death. He'd been older than Alexandra, after all. Frank Rosen was older too, but the age gap wasn't as wide.

Other than the personal connection to terrorists, Rosen's business appeared clean. If he supported the Faction by means unknown, he hid the subterfuge well. But there was no way he didn't know what Alexandra was doing. The Riviera trip wasn't a vacation. He *knew*. They had to look deeper to find out how he supported the Faction. A shell company? Charity of his own? They had yet to discover the link, but it was there...somewhere.

The toaster bell dinged. Reema left the stool and put dinner on a plate and poured a glass of wine.

* * *

Kara pretended to fish. She brought real bait and cast her line like a pro.

She braced herself at the bow and wore a red bikini top and denim cutoffs with her blonde hair tied back. Sunglasses, ball cap—she had the full stereotypical costume. The perfect distraction. She'd get attention, and nobody would wonder who else was aboard. While she tended to her line, Slayton remained out of view in the galley. They'd anchored 200 yards off the coast, and bobbed up and down with the waves within view of Alexandra Ruhl's villa.

Slayton watched the villa through powerful binoculars. He had a notebook and pen to keep track of comings and goings—and there was a lot of movement to watch. At first, he only counted one guard, a big blond bruiser in a black suit. He spotted Alexandra sunbathing by the pool. She didn't look as good in her bikini as Kara did, but Slayton planned to keep mum on both opinions. Frank Rosen appeared at the back door to say something to Alexandra. He didn't stay long before retreating inside once more. With only one soldier present, it seemed to Slayton like a no-brainer to hop over the wall—with Kara—and shoot it out. Giving Alexandra too much time and too long a leash would only help her. She'd get away, activate another sleeper cell, and kill more innocent people. She looked worry free on the lounge chair as she let the suntan her pale body. It pissed Slayton off. She behaved as if she had an ace hidden. The possibility kept Slayton from hopping over the wall with guns blazing. He needed to find what he was missing. He had no idea what he needed to look for.

Thoughts of Reema under threat intruded, too. He could only focus on the problem in front of him. He hated not being at home.

What the hell is she waiting for???

"Woo hoo!" Kara yelled. "Got a big one!"

Slayton remained in position. Kara was displaying more excitement than he'd seen before. He should have started their association with a fishing trip.

"Jack, come see!"

He didn't move.

"Jack?"

He stayed in place. Watching. A splash indicated she'd tossed the fish back into the water. There was no stove in their hotel room to cook anything she caught. And he didn't relish the idea of a nighttime cooking adventure on the beach either.

And then...

Two black SUVs stopped at the villa's gate. The gate swung open, and the blond bruiser in black waited on the porch. The SUVs traveled up the drive and stopped. Four men climbed out of each vehicle and unloaded several large cases. They carried the cases into the house.

"Bingo."

Shooters and their guns. Now Alexandra had the protection he'd expected. The force meant she planned to stay for a while. But for what?

Slayton spent a moment updating his notes. He'd call home base with the update. They were going to need more help for sure.

"Jack?"

Kara stood in the galley doorway.

"What?"

"You alive in there?"

"Busy, Kara."

"I took a picture of the fish! It was bigger than my head!"

"How exciting," he said. He didn't turn his head to see her. He was still looking at the villa.

* * *

Reema drove to work with the passenger windows cracked to let the morning air inside. She glanced at the dash clock. 7:45 a.m. Traffic on the Dulles Toll Road conspired to make her late. Mason wouldn't be happy.

She wasn't sure even Superman could give her a clear lane. Brake lights formed a red river, moving inch by inch. Accident? Roadwork? Didn't matter. She fished her phone from her purse. Before she hit Mason's number, the phone buzzed with a text alert. The display read "Old Buzzard."

Where are you? Briefing in 15.

Reema texted back her situation.

Move faster. Find a way.

"You son of a bitch," she muttered. Reema set the phone down and scrolled through the map of her in-dash GPS. A detour—exit onto Route 7, pick up the back roads, and rejoin the freeway. Problem was she wouldn't be the only one. It might take fifteen minutes to reach said exit as well. But it didn't, and the ramp wasn't as crowded as she'd thought. She accelerated with a short line of cars. The trees lining the route blurred into a green haze. The tension in her neck and shoulders eased. But then, in her rearview mirror, she noticed a gray sedan. The driver hung back a few car lengths but matched her speed.

It's another commuter...

Wait. I saw that car earlier!

Reema first noticed the gray Toyota at Starbucks when she picked up her morning fix. One man driving, dressed in jeans and a wrinkled T-shirt, very lean with sharp blue eyes. Remembering Jack's warning, she changed her route to the office. She didn't often use the toll road, yet here was the gray Camry once more.

Paranoia? Sure. But nothing they knew about the New Red Army Faction suggested they had any amateurs in the ranks.

Reema decided to test the situation. She stepped harder on the accelerator. Only a little. She had two car lengths between her and the van ahead. She changed lanes, moving into the right, speeding up to pass the van. She corrected at the last second and made a sharp right turn onto a side street. Her tires chirped. She straightened and slowed. Suburban homes with manicured lawns lined either side. Reema looked ahead but watched the rearview too.

She executed the textbook evasion protocols. Vary speed. Unexpected turns. Create distance.

Another glance in the rearview. The gray Toyota grew in size as it followed after her. Not a coincidence.

Yellow light.

Reema hit the brakes too hard, and her tires protested with a brief screech but she made the stop. The gray Camry slowed. Reema's pulse only spiked a little. Combat wasn't new to her. Neither was almost dying.

The light changed, and Reema veered left across opposing lanes. She drove into a small shopping complex, circled the lot, and backed into a parking slot beside a dumpster. It gave her a little cover from the parking entrance—if the Camry followed, he wouldn't spot her right away. Meanwhile, she had a decent view. The Camry's driver hesitated at the entrance, then a car behind him honked, and the driver turned into the lot. Reema had her phone camera going, zooming in on the Camry. Tinted windows prevented her from seeing the driver. But as the Camry U-turned and went out the way it came, she caught the license plate. Not a rental. Stolen? Worst case, stolen, yeah. Useless. But maybe they could still get a lead.

Reema stayed put long enough to get her breathing back to normal and update Mason. His reply assured her he understood the problem.

Be careful. Get here when you can.

Mason could be a real prick, she decided, but he wasn't all bad. The problem was nobody ever knew which version of him they were going to get at any one time.

35

Reema merged back onto the highway. The detour had two benefits. She exposed the tail and cleared the backup. Nobody else followed her, and by 9:45 a.m., she was clearing the security gate and turning into the employee parking lot.

The bull pen hummed with activity. She ignored the noise and didn't bother to stop at her office. She went straight to Nathan Mason. He looked up from his paperwork as she entered without knocking.

"Tail confirmed?" he asked. Alarm filled his expression.

"Yes," she said, setting her laptop case on a chair. "I have him on video. Phone's in the car, though."

Headquarters had a ban on cell phones inside the building. Zero exceptions.

"Get the driver?"

"Tinted windows. No."

"Stolen car. No good to us."

"What about you?" Reema remained standing. "Jack said—"

"I remember what Jack told us," Mason said. He glanced at the bullpen and a group of analysts huddled around a desk screen. "I haven't noticed anything on my end."

Reema wondered, *Are you even looking?* The CIA, as one author once put it, was like a post office, but with spies. Nobody at HQ ever considered they'd be in danger.

"We need outside help," Mason said.

"Like Jack suggested."

"Like Jack suggested," Mason responded. "My predecessor, right?"

"Dylan Sharp, yes. I have him on speed dial."

"Do it. Tell him we need eyes on our six. And send *him* your video. This kill team could be stealing cars near their hideout. Keep *our* people out of this. We don't know how far Alexandra Ruhl managed to reach."

Reema left Mason's office. Weaving through the bullpen, she felt the weight of unseen eyes, and none of them belonged to her coworkers. But she wasn't alone this time. Not at all. Even with Jack gone, she had help, close by, ready to respond.

* * *

During lunch, Reema headed to her car to use her cell phone. The Agency's "no cell phone" rule prevented hacked devices from recording or eavesdropping. The rule made sense but came with a humorous consequence. Dozens of CIA employees flooded the parking lot every day at lunch time, each retreating to their cars for the same reason. The sight was so entertaining that a second group of employees often gathered to observe the daily exodus. Everybody chuckled at the shared ritual.

Reema and Jack stayed in regular contact with their former boss, Dylan Sharp. His close bond with Jack remained strong despite Dylan's departure from CIA. Dylan's exit was no surprise, given what they went through during the October Blood debacle. His decision to lead the private military company embroiled in the scandal, however, had left many shocked. Dylan insisted he took the role to restore the company's reputation, claiming it had a strong track record of handling national security contracts despite the misdeeds of its former management.

She dialed Dylan's personal number. He answered after two rings.

"Reema? Everything all right?"

If it wasn't Jack calling him, Dylan thought he was dead or in trouble. His concern had merit, though. Everything was not all right.

"We're fine. Sort of."

"Tell me more."

"Jack is overseas, and the threat has come ashore. I'm a target. So is Nathan Mason. We need your help, Dylan. Discreet surveillance. Possible threat assessment. Can you meet me?"

"You can't use your own resources?"

"We have our reasons."

"I get it. Usual spot, tonight, seven o'clock."

"I'll be there. I also have a video for you to check out."

"Send it."

"On the way. Thank you, Dylan."

"Anytime."

Reema ended the call and forwarded her video of the gray Camry. She hesitated for a moment because the dead end had neon lights. There was more than one on the kill team, and they'd use a different car next time. But how many leads looked like dead ends at first, only to pay off? Enough to always try, she decided. She sent the video. Her stomach grumbled. She put the phone back in the glove box and left her car. Time for a sandwich and salad in the commissary. Or, hell with it. She'd go for a double cheeseburger instead.

* * *

DYLAN SHARP FROWNED at his chipped coffee mug. The brew had gone cold. Had he been staring at the computer monitor longer than he realized?

The former manager of Z Section, and now head of the Eagle Alliance, placed the mug on his desk. He regarded the list of names on his screen once more. He had three operatives to spare to assist Reema and Mason. Dylan didn't know Mason well. They'd only coordinated during the transition when Dylan was exiting CIA for good. He couldn't handle being there after a betrayal that literally altered the course of his life. Taking over the Eagle Alliance at the center of the scandal related to the betrayal didn't seem any better. He wanted to make the Eagle Alliance a shining example of how to do it right. And he wanted to redeem himself for missing the signs he should have noticed but didn't because he'd been in love with the woman who destroyed everything.

And the Eagle Alliance saw him as a reformer. At the CIA, true or not, he felt like a failure and was sure many more agreed. He couldn't work under such a cloud.

Dylan noticed his three picks were on rotation at Eagle's training facility. They had no current mission. He phoned the center to tell them he was on his way. He had a better gig for his guys than shooting static targets.

* * *

TUCKED AWAY in a forgotten corner of the Blue Ridge Mountains, the Eagle Alliance training facility was a fortress of secrecy. Barbed wire fences, motion sensors, and patrols kept prying eyes at bay. The air was crisp and clean but smelled of pine and gunfire. It was a familiar cocktail for men like Eliot Hawk, Simon Gonzales, and Tate Matthews.

All three were experts from military SpecOps. Hawk came from Delta Force, Gonzales a former Green Beret. Matthews was the ex-Navy SEAL turned legend in the shadows. SpecOps assignments weren't forever, and the fire in their veins hadn't cooled by the time honorable discharge reared its head. They traded government paychecks for the private sector's fat contracts.

Eliot Hawk, the team leader, stood at the edge of the mock-up building. It was a squat, single-level structure pieced together from shipping containers and plywood and designed to mimic the labyrinthine interiors of urban hideouts or terrorist compounds.

At forty-two, Hawk was the oldest, his face etched with lines from too many ops. He scanned the entry point: a reinforced door on the east side. "All right, gents," he said, his voice a low rumble. "This ain't Baghdad or Kabul. No real bullets, but the timer's real. Eight minutes to clear. ID hostiles, neutralize 'em, extract any friendlies, and punch out the west exit. If we get turned around in the maze and come out the way we came in, it's an automatic fail."

Simon Gonzales chuckled, slapping a magazine into his training carbine loaded with simunition rounds, paint markers that hit hard but left you breathing. At thirty-five, Gonzales was the team's breacher and medic. He was built like a tank, broad and thick, the result of spending more time at the gym than at the bar.

Tate Matthews, the youngest at thirty-two, leaned against the wall, his lanky frame coiled like a spring. He was the sniper and scout, eyes always darting, fingers twitching near his sidearm.

Hawk checked his watch. The digital timer on the facility's control tower blinked red. 00:00. "Stack up. Gonzales, you're on point for breach. Matthews, cover our six."

The buzzer sounded, and the timer started. Gonzales kicked the door with practiced force, the frame splintering under his boot. They poured in, M-4 carbines raised, sweeping the first room in a fluid CQB formation. The interior was a disorienting warren of narrow corridors, false walls, and dead ends. Flickering fluorescent bulbs buzzed loudly. Cardboard cutouts representing armed hostiles or terrified hostages were rigged to pop up at random.

"Clear left," Gonzales whispered, sweeping the corner with his weapon. A hostile dummy erupted from behind a crate, AK-47 silhouette in hand. Gonzales fired twice, the paint splattering red across the target's chest. "Tango down."

Hawk nodded, advancing. "Good shot. Push forward." The maze twisted right, then left, forcing them to double back once already. Graffiti and mock propaganda posters plastered the walls, adding to the immersion. Sweat beaded on Hawk's brow.

They hit the first T-intersection with doors on either

side. Matthews covered the rear, his breathing steady. "Movement behind—wait, false alarm."

"Stay sharp," Hawk said. "Gonzales, take the right door. I'll cover."

Gonzales nudged the door open with his muzzle. Inside, a mock living quarters: overturned furniture, dim lighting. Two dummies popped up—one a woman in a hijab clutching a child (hostage), the other a bearded man with a pistol. Gonzales hesitated a split second, then fired at the gunman. Paint bloomed on the hostile's torso. "Hostage safe. Clear."

But as they exited, the maze played its trick. The corridor looped, disorienting with identical turns. Hawk glanced at the faint markings on the floor. Arrows meant to mislead. "This way's north...no, west. Damn it, orient on the exit vector."

Timer: 03:12.

Deeper in, the challenges ramped up. They entered a larger chamber simulating a command center. Wires dangled from the ceiling like vines. Three hostiles sprang up in quick succession. One from behind a desk, another from a doorway, the third camouflaged against the wall. Matthews yelled, "Contact right!" He dropped the wall-hugger with a precise shot, but the desk guy clipped Gonzales's vest with a simulated round, paint grazing his shoulder.

"Shit!" Gonzales grunted, rubbing the spot. It stung, but he pushed on. "I'm good. Keep moving."

Hawk took the doorway hostile, two rounds center mass. "You hit?"

"Love tap," Gonzales said through gritted teeth.

The team pressed on. The maze narrowed into a choke

point. Hallway lined with doors, each potentially a trap. As they advanced, doors flew open. Hostiles mixed with hostages: a kid dummy, an armed militant, a civilian cowering.

"Prioritize!" Hawk barked. Gonzales cleared left, nailing a hostile mid-draw. Matthews swept right, holding fire on a hostage while popping the one behind her. Hawk centered, dropping two in rapid succession. But in the chaos, Gonzales got turned around, facing a dead end.

"Dead end! Backtrack!" Gonzales called.

Timer: 05:27.

Panic edged in. The maze punished hesitation, with false exits leading back to the start.

Hawk grabbed Gonzales's shoulder. "On me. Tate, map it in your head. You've got the eyes for this."

Matthews nodded, his mind racing. As the scout, he'd memorized the briefing blueprint, but the live run twisted it. "Left at the next fork, then sharp right. Avoid the loop."

They hustled, boots echoing on the concrete floor. Another room: a mock interrogation cell. A hostage dummy chained to a chair, flanked by two guards. One guard popped up firing. Sim rounds whizzing past Hawk's ear. He fired, paint marking the target. Gonzales freed the "hostage" by cutting a zip tie with his knife, while Matthews covered the door.

"Hostage secured. Simulate extract," Gonzales said, hoisting the dummy over his shoulder like a sack.

But the exit path branched again. A wrong turn loomed —a corridor curving back east, toward the entry. Hawk felt the disorientation hit. "Which way?"

Matthews paused, eyes narrowing. "Straight through that wall panel. It's a false one."

Gonzales bashed it with his shoulder, revealing a hidden passage. "Nice call, Tate. I'd have looped us."

Timer: 06:45.

Adrenaline surged as they navigated the final stretch. It was a gauntlet of rapid-fire pop-ups. Hostiles everywhere. One leaping from above, another from a vent. Hawk took a hit to the leg, the paint splatter leaving a sting, but he stayed on target and dropped his assailant with a double-tap of return fire. If only cardboard could feel the same sting he did.

"Cover me!" Hawk yelled, suppressing a groan.

Gonzales laid down fire, neutralizing two more. "Boss down! Matthews, flank!"

Matthews darted left, his shots precise, clearing the path. "Path open! Move, move!"

They burst into the last chamber, a storage room with the west exit in sight. One final hostile—a sniper dummy in the rafters. It "fired," clipping Matthews's arm. He winced but returned fire, the paint hitting true.

"Clear!" Matthews shouted.

They staggered through the west door as the timer hit 07:58. The buzzer blared. Success.

Outside, the Virginia air felt like freedom. They collapsed against the wall, laughing through the wear and tear. Paint marked their gear like badges of honor.

Matthews wiped sweat from his brow. "Next time, let's make it six minutes. Keep it interesting."

"Are you nuts?" said Hawk.

"Are you scared?" Matthews said.

Another man wearing an instructor's uniform approached with a satisfied smile. "Good work, boys."

The three men stood because the second man with the instructor was his boss. "Hey. Look what the wind blew in."

Dylan Sharp smiled and shook hands with the three operators.

The instructor said, "The boss says he needs you, and since he signs my check, I gotta do what he says, right?"

Hawk frowned at Dylan. "We got a mission?"

"A small one. And it's local," Dylan explained. "Why don't you guys get cleaned up and we can talk about it. We start tonight."

36

"NATE! I FOUND WHY THEY'RE IN SAINT-TROPEZ."

Reema spoke with a rush of excitement as she set her laptop on the edge of Mason's desk. The older man frowned. If she saw him working on something else, as he was, she didn't show any sign. Her lack of a phone call advising him of her visit irked him. Such was the life of management. She noticed the look on his face, and he noticed she didn't care. Which meant her discovery was worth an interruption, and he needed to pay attention.

"All right, what?"

She sat and spoke as she consulted the laptop screen.

"They hired a plastic surgeon in Vienna. The doctor has a flight booked for Saint-Tropez."

The lines on Mason's face tightened. "Is this all?"

"It explains why we lost them in Vienna. She wants to change her face."

"Doesn't explain why she's hiding in the open, though."

"Jack's theory?"

Mason scoffed. "She can't change her face," he continued. "The idea is stupid."

"The doctor is Hannes Hoferle," Reema said. She turned the laptop toward Mason. "He caters to celebrities, oligarchs dodging sanctions, stuff like that. The timing matches their Vienna detour."

"Yes, yes, you made that clear."

"Now, Alexandra can't erase her face all the way, but subtle changes? Cheek implants, nose refinement, brow lift. It would be enough to throw off facial recognition. Nate, she could slip into deep cover, and we'll never find her again."

"She's not unattractive, though," Mason said. "Her vanity—"

"Overridden by survival. She's already hit the wall and at the age where getting work done is a natural choice."

"Hit the wall?"

"It means she's getting old, and men won't pay attention to her."

Mason blinked. "You women are ruthless." He didn't wait for her reply. His attention went to her notes on the screen. "Did Frank Rosen pay the doctor?"

"It was Rosen's accounts that led us to this, and Rosen is playing sugar daddy. But I'd bet she has an emergency fund equal to a small country's budget. She'll use those funds for living expenses."

Mason leaned closer to see the numbers and other data Reema compiled. Crunching numbers was never his strong suit. The typed summaries on another page spelled out the details he needed.

"This says he's routing his big pharma profits to crypto wallets. Did he use crypto for Vienna?"

Reema nodded.

"Did he move any more money? Pay the assassins allegedly tracking you and me?"

"No evidence at this time."

Mason leaned back in his chair. "When do you see Sharp?"

"Tonight." Reema took back the laptop and closed the lid.

Whatever Mason planned to say next never left his mouth. The ringing phone interrupted his thoughts. He snatched the receiver.

"Yes?" Pause. "Hang on, Jack."

Reema's face brightened. Mason turned on the speaker-phone and put the handset down.

"Jack," he said, louder, "you're on with me and Reema. What's the word?"

"It's heating up," Slayton responded. "Kara and I have the villa locked down visually. They're fortifying on the other side of the walls."

"How?" Mason asked.

Slayton explained the arrival of the new gunmen. "They're staying in the house, and they have drones to scan the property."

"Ruhl is expecting a plastic surgeon they hired in Vienna."

"Which means she may stay put for a while."

Reema said, "We have a trace on the doctor, Jack. We'll let you know when he leaves Vienna."

"We'll hold position," Slayton said, "but this doctor gives me an idea. We're going to need more help."

"On the way," Mason said.

"What about you two?"

Reema told Slayton about her morning and upcoming meeting with Dylan Sharp.

"Neither of you go home tonight," Slayton said when she finished.

"Way ahead of you, babe," Reema said.

"Whose credit card are you using?"

"Yours, of course."

"Nuts. You make more than me."

"Enough!" Mason snapped. "Jack, stand by for notice on the doctor and backup."

"Talk soon."

The line clicked. Maston turned off the phone with a scowl. He glared at Reema. "The two of you—"

"I'm going back to work," Reema said. She departed before he said more, but didn't hide her smile.

Mason sighed. He glanced at the phone. He supposed they needed a little levity considering the situation. But he didn't have the talent to create any. He resumed work as well. The net was tightening on both ends, and they had a long day still to go.

* * *

DYLAN'S "USUAL SPOT" was a small restaurant near the offices of the Eagle Alliance. The smell of strong coffee and frying food mingled with canned '80s pop. Reema's senses were elsewhere. She scanned like sonar, attempting to detect a threat before it had a moment to take shape.

She sat in a far corner booth, back to the wall. Random decorations covered stained and faded wallpaper somebody should have replaced decades ago. Her shoulders kept tensing. She had to make a conscious effort to stay loose. Her eyes shifted to the door every time it opened, and she sized up every customer as they waited for a table. She checked faces for signs of hostility. She watched their posture for "tells" of a man or woman prepared to fight or packing weapons. She caught almost every subtle movement around her, too. A man fidgeting with a Zippo lighter as he listened to the whispers of an intense female companion. A woman alone staring at the menu but also pulling at her hair. A group of young adults laughing in the opposite corner. And she had to tell herself to quit. She was doing a number on her nerves. She'd be a frightened wreck by the end of the night if she didn't stop.

The door swung open again and gave off its soft chime. She zeroed on the new arrival and sighed with relief. Dylan Sharp had finally shown up. He wasn't late, but the tension Reema felt in her gut made it seem like his joining her took longer than it should. He wore casual clothes and spotted her before one of the waitresses had a chance to intercept him. He weaved through to her table and smiled as he slid into the booth opposite.

"How are you, Reema? It's been a few months."

"New boss keeps us hopping," she said. "And I hate to only call you because we have a problem."

"I'm here for whatever you need."

Reema smiled back. Her coffee had gone cold, so when the waitress arrived to ask Dylan what he wanted, Reema also asked for a refill. They ordered food at the same time.

"I'll let the leftovers sit another night," she said.

"It's funny what you can save when Jack isn't around."

She laughed.

"How is he?"

She noted Dylan had the sense not to ask, “Where is he?” but then of course he would.

“As far as I know, very well. Getting some sun the last few days.”

“And related to his current whereabouts—”

“The other side has sent people after me and Mason,” she said. She explained further without giving away mission secrets. They paused only when their waitress brought the coffee.

“Your video didn’t give us anything to work with,” he told her.

“We thought so.” Reema stirred sugar into her coffee.

“I have three guys to help,” Dylan said.

“Mason said he’d pay you off the books, but three—”

“He’s that much of a hard ass?”

“We call him Old Buzzard. But he’s fair. Usually backs us up when it matters.”

“It *always* matters.”

“He has a different style of management than you, for sure.”

“Are you staying at home?”

“Are you kidding?”

“I figured not,” he said. “But?”

“I have emergency clothes and things in the trunk of my car, but if this goes more than a few days we’ll need to go back for more.”

“Fair enough.” He swallowed some coffee. “You carrying?”

“Glock in my purse.”

“Better to have it and not need it.”

“Yup,” she agreed. “All right. With you and three others, what’s your plan?”

"Countersurveillance. Track them tracking you and see where they hide. Maybe get them first."

"We're not interested in taking them alive, Dylan."

"If Jack gets rid of their leader—"

"I didn't say anything about what Jack is doing."

"Come on, Reema."

She shrugged.

"But really. If he—"

"I don't think there's any communication between the parties. The kill team is on autopilot."

"Then do I need to ask my next questions?"

"What?" she said.

"Will another team take their place?"

"Not if Jack does his part."

"Good."

The waitress arrived with their food. Reema dug in. She hadn't realized how hungry she was.

37

SLAYTON HAD TO WORK HARD AT STAYING FOCUSED. HIS THOUGHTS wandered often to Reema being in danger back home.

Kara Botticker tried to help.

"Your lover will be fine."

"You think so?"

"After what you told me of her previous adventures, I don't see how she could be in any danger at all. Plus, you said she has help."

"She does."

"She'll be fine."

"Anybody waiting for you at home, Kara?"

"Um...no."

"I can tell."

Kara frowned, and her eyes narrowed, and if she'd been free to murder him, Slayton felt certain she would have.

Slayton apologized and let it drop. But she didn't understand the frustration and anger over not being with Reema. It reminded him of the three years he thought she'd died in action while undercover. The fact she survived proved Kara's point, though. Reema wasn't a weak woman by any means.

"By the way," Kara said, "I notice you don't seem as worried about your boss."

"You do?"

Kara offered only the third smile he'd seen across her face.

The mid-afternoon sun glinted off the tarmac at the Aeroport du Golfe Saint-Tropez and cast a long shadow from the private jet parked near one of the outer hangars. A customs crew was busy checking luggage and equipment and passports. Slayton and Kara watched from their vehicle outside the fence.

"The doctor doesn't look happy," Kara said. She watched through binoculars.

"I think he expected his client to grease the skids a little."

"What do you mean?"

"Bribe customs."

Dr. Hannes Hoferle had a small entourage with him. Along with carry-on luggage, they brought large cases of medical equipment from the jet. The doctor had to explain every piece to the customs agents who then made notes on clipboards.

Slayton's gaze shifted to the big vehicles at the hangar doors. Two black SUVs with sunlight reflecting off the faux-chrome trim. Slayton and Kara had seen the SUVs before. Alexandra Ruhl's backup arrived in those same SUVs two days ago when they'd watched from their boat.

The help provided by Mason arrived twenty-four hours earlier. Mason sent a group of operators from CIA's Ground Branch, pulled away from a training mission with the

British SAS. They were happy to do some real fighting beside Slayton and Kara. Slayton hoped they were a cut above some of the Ground Branch operators he knew, like the fuck-offs from SOF units nobody wanted around. Grand Branch had far too many of those. Sometimes it showed.

Slayton radioed the support team to tell them Dr. Hoferle had yet to start moving.

They had a plan for intercepting Hoferle, but it was a rushed plan. Slayton didn't like to rush. Sometimes, there wasn't a choice. You assembled a plan based on experience and what you had to work with in the moment. The first part of the plan required a daytime strike. Slayton would have preferred not to do something so public because it would bring the attention of the police. But he wanted to hit before Hoferle arrived at the villa. He didn't want civilians in the line of fire. With the Ground Branch team, they'd set up a safe house to hold the doctor and his crew while they took care of the dirty work at the villa. For the plan to work, he needed to hijack the doctor's caravan before they reached the villa.

"Looks like they got the all clear," Kara said.

Hoferle and his entourage split between the two SUVs. The doctor and another man holding a stainless-steel briefcase climbed into the lead vehicle. The rest with their larger cases took the second. Alexandra's men—a driver and shotgun passenger for each vehicle—started the engines. Tires crunched over asphalt as they pulled away from the hangar, turned left out of sight around the opposite side, then appeared again to pass through an automated gate onto the street.

Slayton waited, counting down the seconds until the SUVs merged onto the road. Slayton started his car and put it in gear. Kara radioed the Ground Branch team and turned in her seat to look back.

"They're behind us," she said.

"Uh-huh." Slayton keyed his own handheld radio to talk to the support team. "Move on my mark. We'll only get one chance."

Slayton set down the radio and felt silly for telling the team what they already knew. The team leader acknowledged, and Slayton locked on the taillights of the SUVs ahead. He felt the weight of the mission pressing against his chest. How much of the pressure came from knowing Reema had a kill team looking for her? Whether they succeeded in Saint-Tropez determined if she lived or died, too.

They had one chance to finish Alexandra Ruhl.

Then Slayton needed to get home.

* * *

Dr. Hannes Hoferle stepped from the private jet's narrow stairs and appeared pleased. They'd had an easy flight but now he was ready to work. Behind him, his four assistants followed. They held two large cases packed with surgical equipment. One held a sleek stainless-steel briefcase holding the doctor's custom tools.

Customs agents met them and not only checked their papers but the gear, too. They took a long time, and Hoferle's patience wore thin very fast.

The four men sent by Alexandra Ruhl stood waiting by their black Mercedes SUVs. They looked like trouble. The men were all broad-shouldered with hard faces, one with a noticeable scar. They weren't chauffeurs, Hoferle knew.

Perhaps this is a mistake. But as he and his people approached the waiting SUVs, Hoferle knew he had no choice. Ruhl's companion paid in advance. And Alexandra's errand boys looked like the type who could snap necks without blinking. Still, he assured himself, and felt strange for doing so, they meant no harm. To someone else, yes, he was sure, but not him. And not yet. It was the *not yet* that bothered him most.

The Germans moved forward and helped his assistants load the cases into the SUVs. Hoferle noted how they handled the gear with care. They faced their own consequences if they broke anything. He finally climbed into the lead SUV and settled into the leather seat. Karl, his number two, the keeper of the custom tools in the stainless-steel briefcase, sat beside him. The other assistants filed into the second vehicle.

The driver was stone-faced with a buzz cut and said nothing. His hands remained steady on the wheel as the engine hummed to life, and he started driving away.

The German in the passenger seat, a jagged scar across his left cheek, turned to him.

"Frau Ruhl is waiting," the man said. "She wants you to start the surgery as soon as possible."

Hoferle's lips pressed into a thin line. "We need to do our prep work, and none of it happens fast. We will complete the job, but we will not rush the job. I told Frau Ruhl this in Vienna."

"Not my concern. I'm only passing on what she said."

"Perhaps Frau Ruhl should keep her mouth shut from time to time."

The German let out a bark of laughter. The driver did not. Falling silent once more, he faced forward.

"Where did you get the scar?" the doctor asked.

"Knife fight. Long time ago."

"Want it fixed?" the doctor asked.

"I find women like it." The German turned and grinned at him.

Hoferle sat back. He exchanged glances with Karl, who shrugged. Then he thought about the job. Alexandra wanted her face altered and her identity erased. Hoferle explained what she wanted wasn't possible. Subtle changes, yes, much more realistic. Using charts, he showed her how he could alter her nose and cheekbones, soften her jawline, a few other things. She seemed to agree, but he wondered if she'd bring up the argument a second time. And use threats of violence if he didn't comply.

I'm making this worse by thinking too much. Shut up!

The SUV hummed along the coastal road. The Mediterranean glittered to his right, and he turned his attention there instead. Always better to ponder beauty over ugliness.

The driver's voice destroyed the silence. He screamed loud and raw.

"*Achtung*!"

38

DR. HOFERLE'S HEART POUNDED AS THE SUV LURCHED TO A STOP, the screech of the tires filling the cabin. A sedan cut in front of them, turning perpendicular to the road. Metal crunched as the SUV smashed into the sedan. And then Hoferle and Karl screamed like children as a man and a woman, both holding guns, emerged from the sedan. The gun muzzles glinted with lethal intent. Their steady eyes meant they knew how to shoot with great efficiency. His stomach twisted. This wasn't right. Alexandra sent men to protect them, yet they were still targets.

The driver cursed, fumbling for a handgun, but the world exploded before he put his weapon into action. Two sharp cracks shattered the windshield. Glass exploded inward in a spray of jagged shards. The driver's head snapped back, and blood splattered across the dash. He slumped and his head landed on the horn. The blaring wail drowned out Hoferle and Karl's screams as they dove for the floor.

He was a surgeon, not a soldier. Bullets weren't part of

his life! Alexandra's lucrative offer had blinded him. Now, he regretted ever speaking to her.

* * *

SLAYTON'S LIFTED the handheld radio to his mouth.

"Now!"

And he hit the accelerator.

The sedan roared forward, engine snarling, overtaking the two SUVs in a blur. Kara braced for what happened next. Slayton wrenched the wheel. The sedan skidded. Tires shrieked. The vehicle skewed sideways to block the narrow road. The first SUV's driver reacted too late. More rubber screeched on the asphalt. The stench of scorched tires and brakes filled the air. The SUV jolted to a stop with its bumper kissing the sedan's rear passenger door with a crunch. Dust billowed, obscuring the road in a hazy cloud.

The Ground Branch team in Slayton's backup car acted at the same time. One operative leaned out the passenger side and blasted the rear tires of the second SUV. The tires exploded, rubber shredding into black ribbons. The SUV lurched, its driver wrestling the wheel as the back fishtailed. The vehicle veered toward the roadside. It slammed to a stop against a low barrier. The Ground Branch crew leaped from their vehicle and swarmed the wreck.

Slayton and Kara exited their sedan in a hurry, too. Slayton's gun sights settled on the SUV's windshield, the driver frozen in panic. He fired twice, punching through the glass, turning it in a mosaic of cracks. Blood sprayed the dashboard from the new holes in the driver's face. He slumped forward, the horn blaring in a long wail as the body came to rest on the wheel.

The passenger door opened, and Scarface jumped out with an HK machine pistol. Slayton was faster. Two more rounds from the CZ nine-millimeter punched through the German's chest. The killer staggered, eyes wide with shock, the HK falling from his grasp and his body doing likewise.

Kara sprinted to the SUV's rear door, wrenching it open with a grunt. Inside, Dr. Hoferle cowered on the floor, arms shielding his head. Karl, with the briefcase, held the stainless-steel container in front of him as a shield.

Kara leaned in to grab the doctor's collar. He gasped, eyes darting back and forth, as she pressed her gun's muzzle against the soft flesh under his ear. "You'll live as long as you do what we say," she said.

Hoferle nodded. Sweat beaded on his brow. He lifted trembling hands in surrender.

Slayton pivoted to the Ground Branch crew. They had descended on the second SUV. The vehicle was a wreck, one side lodged against a barrier, doors open. Two Germans kneeled on the gravel, hands zip-tied behind their backs. Hoferle's assistants stood frozen, hands raised, staring down gun barrels.

Slayton said into the radio, "We're running out of time."

"Targets secured," one of the CIA team, Ramirez, radioed back. "Ready to move."

Slayton raised a fist. The CIA backup team hauled their prisoners to their feet and shoved them back into the SUV. The Germans took to their original vehicle. Some of the CIA crew rode in the second SUV as well. Slayton knew this next part would get sticky. They had to use the enemy's vehicles to try and fool home base, and he'd blasted out the window of one of them.

Kara climbed in beside Hoferle and his still-cowering second hand, Karl. She grinned at Karl, who responded with a gasp. Slayton pulled the dead driver out and took his seat. He ignored the blood on the wheel, dash, and seat—there'd be plenty of blood to go around in a little while. They peeled out, tires kicking up dust as they barreled toward Alexandra Ruhl's villa.

* * *

Hoferle said, "Please, this is madness! I am not part of whatever this is!"

"The hell you aren't, Doctor," Slayton said.

Hoferle wanted to plead some more, but a glare from Kara made him quiet again. Karl clutched the briefcase to his chest like it was a teddy bear.

The next hour made Hoferle wonder if he was in the Twilight Zone. He'd heard people say something similar while making a joke, but now he understood why. Nothing seemed real. He kept looking around with wide eyes and a frantic pulse.

The people, these men and one woman, with guns and bad attitudes, brought him and his assistants to a secluded cottage near the ocean. Two more men with guns were already at the cottage and told the doctor and his staff to get comfortable and all their needs would be taken care of. The only condition was they couldn't leave or use their phones. The men collected their phones and any other devices, and their bags were set aside in another room and the door locked. Other than no access to their belongings or the ability to move freely, they could do whatever they wanted.

Shortly after, the larger group departed and left them in the care of the two who'd greeted them upon arrival.

None of it made any sense.

Hoferle's staff looked to him for guidance, but all he had to offer was a shrug and an assurance that they might as well settle down and wait for whatever happened next.

THE VILLA LOOMED AHEAD under the sunset. It was a sprawling white stucco fortress with terracotta roofing. Palm trees swayed. Slayton slowed at the guard entrance, but there was nobody in the shack. He did see a drone flying toward them, though. He pressed on the gas pedal, and the SUV rushed forward, straining against the wrought-iron electric gate for a moment, before the metal twisted and snapped and either side of the gate flung aside as the SUV crashed through.

Before they left the cottage, Kara said to him, "This had better work."

Slayton only had one reply. "If not, I won't be around long enough to hear you say I told you so."

He was alone in the SUV. Kara was with the Ground Branch team, and they had their attack planned from another direction.

The fight would end quickly if Slayton's idea for a distraction didn't work.

The front of the house loomed large. Stone lions sat on either side of the front steps. The SUV bounced over the rough driveway.

Slayton steered for the lion on the left.

39

Slayton turned sharply as the SUV smashed into the lion and broke more of the battered vehicle. The impact also sent chunks of the lion through the front window, shattering the glass, and onto the lawn. He slid the SUV across the green lawn and stopped with the passenger side facing the house. As he exited, the whine of two overhead drones announced Alexandra's response. Slayton dived flat. Automatic weapons mounted on the drones spit flame, and bullets ripped into the SUV and slapped the ground. Slayton, up and running, zigzagged to avoid the automatic targeting. But the drones followed him around the side of the villa. He cut left and vaulted over a hedge, the impact of landing on hard cement making him cry out. He swallowed the rest of the yell and bit back the pain rising through his body. *Ugh! Next time, look where you're landing, dummy!* The drones, after passing, corrected and moved back at a slower rate of speed.

Slayton fired over the top of the hedge and one drone exploded. The other sped off, firing a burst as it drifted away. Slayton tracked the drone but held back his shot. What he needed was a shotgun...

Alexandra spent half her force collecting Dr. Hoferle. All she had left were four gunners and their drones. How many men did she need to fly the drones? Or were they on autopilot? He decided it didn't matter. He had to find a way to get inside the house and end the fight.

More buzzing. Growing louder. Three drones this time, heading for his position. Slayton fired twice, missing. The drones fired back. The glass behind him shattered, shards raining down on him as he hugged the ground. As the drones closed in, Slayton rose and dived through the broken window behind him. He pulled the curtain down as he entered, rolling on the floor, tangled in the fabric. A salvo from the drones outside ripped into the house. He rolled away, dislodged from the curtain, and let out a short sigh of relief. But he wasn't out of danger at all.

Touching the earbud in his left ear, he said, "Kara, watch out for the drones."

"Copy."

"I'm inside."

"We're one minute out."

* * *

Kara and the Ground Branch team landed at the villa's jetty, jumped out of the boat, and ran to the perimeter. Kara signaled a halt behind a marble fountain where water trickled. One guard was watching and immediately spoke into a radio. Before Kara gave another order, the three drones

Slayton warned about came at them in a sweeping turn. The mounted weapons crackled.

Kara dropped flat, the rest of the team spreading out. Water splashed from bullet impacts. A chunk of the fountain blew off and landed on her back.

Drones have limited ammo, she thought. She fired at the guard at the rear of the house, and he returned the favor before running back inside.

One of the CIA men, armed with a short shotgun, fired a round of double-ought buck. One drone exploded. He fired again at another, missing. The two remaining flying machines retreated.

"Go!" Kara shouted. She ran ahead, the team catching up. She didn't look to see if they were behind her.

* * *

Slayton paused in the doorway with the CZ P-10C in his right fist.

"We're coming in the back," Kara announced.

"Copy. I'm heading upstairs."

"One gunner, first floor, confirmed."

"Copy."

Slayton moved left and advanced toward the opening at the end, leading to a wider room. He stopped at the corner. Staircase. Open floor. Rooms opposite. Another hallway heading for the back of the house. Heavy footsteps. *And shouting.*

Slayton took a knee and waited. The man talking was alerting somebody else to the incoming assault. The German speakers were talking fast. Slayton only caught a few words at a time. But he knew what the conversation meant.

The gunner ran into the room, and Slayton tagged him with a double-tap. The gunner pitched over mid-run and slammed into the tiled floor. He didn't slide. Slayton jammed the CZ into his shoulder harness and retrieved the fallen man's sub gun. Helping himself to a spare magazine, he started up the steps. Whoever waited up there expected somebody to appear. If he hesitated when he realized it wasn't his buddy, Slayton would have a chance to shoot first. The staircase curved to the left, and he held the sub gun up at the landing.

Last step...

A man with blond hair and wearing a black suit yelled from down the hall. He was leaning out of a doorway to watch the stairwell, and he didn't hesitate when he saw Slayton instead of his buddy. He aimed his sub gun from the hip and fired. Slayton dived forward, rolling to the right. The shots stitched the walls. Slayton kicked open a door and went into a room. He fired back, but his unaimed burst did no good.

"The party's upstairs, Kara," Slayton said.

"We'll bring more popcorn."

Another burst chewed up the doorway. Splinters flew in Slayton's face. He fired back. This was a stalemate if he couldn't score a hit. He fired out the sub gun, tossing it aside, and took out the CZ once more. He stuck his head out and pulled back. He needed to see where the enemy was. The gunman responded with a delayed single shot. He was still in the doorway, still between Slayton and something—or somebody—he was willing to die to protect.

* * *

"WHAT DO WE DO?"

Alexandra snapped furious eyes at Frank Rosen. She'd never seen him under fire before. He wasn't going to be much help. She handed him a submachine gun anyway. He examined the weapon with a frown.

"I'm not familiar with this one."

"There's the trigger. Pull it, and it goes bang."

She had her own weapon and a shoulder bag drooping with grenades and tear gas bombs. They were in the upstairs bedroom. Through the windows, they'd watched the incoming strike force shoot down a drone and run across the yard.

"How do we get out of here?" Rosen said.

"If you're going to be deadweight, I'll shoot you myself."

"Alexandra—"

"You follow *me*, that's what you do, Frank. Follow *me*."

She moved to the balcony, checked the yard, and slid open the glass door. Staying low, she further inspected the grounds. They had to get to the jetty where the speedboat waited. The assault team hadn't disabled the boat, as far as she could tell. And they'd left their boat without a guard, which presumably worked. If they had disabled her boat, she could operate theirs. But how to get down from the balcony?

Her last gunman, at the door, had somebody pinned down near the steps. The stalemate wouldn't last long.

Climbing down wasn't an option. They had no ladder or rope, and she wasn't about to tie sheets together when she didn't have enough time. They could swing over the railing, dangle and drop. They risked a sprain at best or a broken ankle at worst doing so.

Beats a bullet in the back, she decided.

And then her time ran to zero.

* * *

SLAYTON SWUNG his gun around the doorway in a two-hand grip. The Faction gunner raised his weapon at the same time. Slayton fired first. The gunman's head snapped back, and he collapsed in the doorway.

In the bedroom, Alexandra gasped as her man hit the floor. She ran back into the room, brushing past a shocked Rosen, and grabbed for the tear gas in her bag. She pulled the pin and held the spoon down.

"Cover me."

Rosen didn't ask questions. He ran to her, into the doorway, firing blind.

Slayton cut right across the hall, then left again. When Rosen fired, he was slipping into another room halfway down and closer to the bedroom at the end of the hall.

As Slayton rose to his feet, his gun in his right hand now, he heard running. Alexandra and Rosen ran past the room, heading for the stairs. Slayton stepped out with his pistol up. Alexandra dropped a circular item about the size of a brick. The cylinder popped and spewed thick white smoke. It wasn't plain smoke, which would have merely been annoying. They'd set off tear gas, and it was another matter indeed.

Slayton slammed the door shut. Some of the white cloud trickled underneath the door. He ran to the window, lifted it open, and looked out. It was a long drop with only a small sloping overhang between the floors.

"They're coming down to you, Kara. Tear gas up here."

Kara didn't respond.

Slayton looked around for a solution. He was in another bedroom, a small one. He grabbed a pillow from the bed and put it against his face. It was hardly ideal. Probably wouldn't work at all. And his eyes remained exposed.

Nothing's perfect.

He flung the door open and ran out.

* * *

ALEXANDRA AND ROSEN reached the bottom of the stairs and moved across the floor to the other hallway. She didn't stop and look at the body on the floor. Rosen saw it and choked back bile. At the hallway, she rolled a grenade as hard as she could. The explosive clattered across the floor to the end. The explosion shook the walls. She fired a burst right after, then gestured for Rosen to follow with another primed grenade in hand.

Kara and the CIA team spread out in the living room with the back doors and windows behind them. When Alexandra's second grenade flew into the room, she yelled, "Get down!" The blast was harder than the first, rattling the room, blowing portions of the walls apart. Alexandra entered and fired her sub gun one-handed, spraying rounds. Rosen followed, firing in the other direction. Kara snapped off a shot and missed. The escaping pair ran through the room and out the back door before Kara or her team raised their heads.

"Jack, she's running."

"Coming to you!"

And Slayton ran through the room and outside.

"You're nuts," Kara said as she and the others regrouped to join the pursuit.

* * *

ALEXANDRA GLANCED BACK as she ran, her face a mask of fury. She didn't slow. Rosen hustled after her, keeping up. His big frame shielded her a little from the pursuit. They dodged between ornamental hedges heading for the fountain and the jetty ahead. Gunfire snapped at them.

She and Rosen reached the fountain and pounded onto the jetty's wooden plank. Rosen shoved her toward the speedboat, a sleek black craft with twin outboard motors.

"Start the engine!" she yelled, turning to fire at the killers in pursuit.

Her salvo drove them to cover, but they weren't going to stop. She stood her ground and fired again, wildly. She'd hit somebody. When the gun clicked empty, she dropped the magazine and slapped in a fresh one. Another burst. The boat's motor rumbled to life with a throaty growl echoing over the water. Alexandra let the sub gun dangle on its sling and started pitching grenades. She didn't throw them very far. One landed in the fountain and destroyed it, debris flying. The others landed nearby, and their blasts tore up the ground. A man was running toward her, breaking off from the group. He clutched only a pistol. He ran at them like a heat-seeking missile.

Alexandra raised her sub gun to fire, but Rosen grabbed her, pulling her into the boat. She fell and yelled. Rosen, at the controls, pulled the throttle into reverse, the water at the back of the boat churning as the blades spun.

Slayton kept running, lungs burning, legs pumping. The boat backed away from the jetty. He fired twice. Rounds chugged into the plank. Alexandra rose once more and tracked him, her bursts chewing the turf, hot lead zipping around him. When her sub gun went silent again, Slayton seized the opportunity. He stopped, still breathing hard, and took a two-hand grip on his gun.

He fired once.

The bullet caught Frank Rosen square in the chest. He jerked back, eyes wide, blood blooming on his shirt. Alexandra screamed and let go of her weapon. His body hit the deck. She pulled another grenade and flung it in Slayton's direction, felt for another—but the bag was empty. She lunged for the controls and spun the wheel, pointing the boat toward the open sea. Pressing the throttle forward, the boat sped away.

"Frank!" she yelled at him. "Frank!" Her scream was raw and primal, swallowed by the sound of the engine and churning water. Bullets peppered the boat but didn't come near her.

Slayton skidded to a halt at the jetty. He fired until the CZ locked open, but the speedboat was accelerating, a dark shape vanishing into the ocean. Kara joined him, breathing hard.

"Our boat!" Kara shouted. She ran. Slayton followed. He told the CIA team to secure the area.

Slayton and Kara vaulted onto their boat, the craft pitching under their weight. Kara slid into the driver's seat and turned the key and grabbed the throttle. The outboards coughed to life with a guttural snarl vibrating through the deck. Backing up, she then shoved the throttle forward, and the boat surged. The bow lifted, slicing through the water, spray exploding from the rear.

Slayton braced against the left side seat, his CZ reloaded. Kara said, "Take this," and passed him her M-4 carbine. The swells rolled high, tossing them up and down. But they held on.

"She has nowhere to go," Slayton yelled. "What does she think she'll accomplish?"

Kara wrestled with the wheel to stay on course. "She's desperate, Jack. Desperate people do stupid things."

The boat lurched over another swell. A splash of water drenched them. Kara cursed under her breath, adjusting the throttle to close the gap. The engines screamed.

"She's faster than us," Slayton pointed out.

"Now is not the time to be negative!"

Slayton shouldered the M-4 and fired twice.

In the speedboat, Alexandra clung to the wheel. The world blurred through tears and her anguish. Her body shook with heavy sobs, and each one tore through her like a blade. Her empire, built on secrets and deception begun by her husband, lay in flames. Running was pointless, a delay of the inevitable, yet here she was, fleeing. She steered into a wide left turn, aiming for Saint-Tropez proper. She might have a chance to vanish there and melt into the crowds. But then what? No safe houses, no allies, nothing to shield her now.

A sharp *ping* snapped her from grief. Bullets smacked the hull, splintering the fiberglass. She whipped her head around. There, closing fast, was the boat the strike team arrived on with only two aboard. Rage surged in Alexandra's chest. She wrenched the wheel hard, spinning the boat in a tight arc. The bow pointed like an arrow at the Americans, and she slammed the throttle to full power. The engines howled, the boat leaping forward.

Slayton steadied himself, the chop making further shooting a gamble. "She's turning!"

"I see it!"

Kara's eyes widened as the speedboat approached, but her hands stayed firm, throttling up to meet the challenge.

Alexandra raised her weapon and pulled the trigger.

Bullets stitched across their hull. One grazed the console and sparks snapped at Kara. Another whined off the rail inches from Slayton. Slayton returned fire. The gap between them closed.

"Coming in hot!" Kara shouted.

Alexandra's sub gun chattered again. Slayton fired back.

"Get us alongside!"

Kara nodded, yanking the wheel right. Their boat slewed, carving a tight arc. The move positioned Alexandra to their port side as she flashed by, close enough to see her wild eyes. Slayton pumped a burst of fire into her chest. Her body arched back, arms flailing, her sub gun flying from her grasp. She stumbled, then fell, splashing into the dark water. The waves swallowed her.

Kara eased off the throttle, the boat slowing and the bow dipping into the swells. She turned the wheel to circle back. She and Slayton scanned the frothy wake where Alexandra had gone under. The sea was merciless. There was no trace of her.

40

PAVLINA PACED THE ROOM.

She and Drewes and Konig had remained "low profile" ever since the CIA lady, Ashraf, spotted Konig following her in a stolen car. Konig's recklessness was something she specifically asked the two men to avoid. Drewes, the smarter one, hadn't been detected while following the old man. To make sure he remained undetected, she'd ordered an end to the surveillance until further notice.

But her two assistants were anxious to complete the mission. They were angry with her for holding them back.

Pavlina paced the room. Her lips were a flat line, eyes glazed with only the occasional blink. She had a lot on her mind, and none of her thoughts matched those of Drewes and Konig. They knew it. She knew it.

Drewes sat at the table, his fingers drumming a restless rhythm, while Konig leaned against the wall, arms crossed, his jaw tight with his frustration on display. They'd been cooped up here for days.

Pavlina's mind wasn't on them. It was on Jacob. Her

son. Her tiny, perfect boy, left behind with her mother. She saw his gummy smile in her dreams and wanted to feel the weight of him in her arms. The thought of him twisted something deep in her chest, a pain sharper than any blade. She'd left him believing she wasn't coming back. She left him thinking her mother and father were the best options for him. It was her duty to mount a final strike for the cause, for her husband's memory. She expected to—maybe wanted to—die in the attempt, to leave this world in a blaze of vengeance. But her resolve was cracking.

She'd told Andreas she wanted *out* of the life, after all.

What was she doing trying to become part of the violence again?

Jacob's face haunted her. His dark eyes, so like his father's, but soft, untainted by violence. But what if...

What if she went back to raise him in peace, far from the blood and betrayal currently consuming her?

The thought felt like betrayal itself. Abandon the mission? Turn her back on her husband? Andreas's face flashed in her mind, his fierce eyes, his voice promising a world remade. The image was clear but fading. They'd believed in the cause together. They'd believed their sacrifices meant something.

But he was gone. The "great revolution" had crumbled into nothing but ashes and regret. What was left to fight for? A ghost? And not only a ghost, but one who'd agreed it was time for the violence to end?

Andreas had wanted to refuse Alexandra's final mission.

Why had *she* decided to accept?

I was angry. My blood was boiling.

But is this really what I want?

Drewes cleared his throat. "We can't sit here forever,

Pavlina. Ashraf and Mason are still out there. We're wasting time."

She turned to him. Her face remained stoic. "You think I want to be here, hiding like a rat?"

"Then let's get it done!" Konig snapped, pushing off the wall. "We know where Ashraf is. We can take her out tonight, Mason too. End this."

"No," Pavlina said, her voice low but firm. "Not yet. We move when I say, not before."

"You're losing your nerve."

"Enough," she said. "You don't get to question me, Konig. Not after you nearly got us all burned."

He glared at her, but she held his gaze, unyielding. Drewes shifted in his chair. "Pavlina," he said carefully, "we trust you. But Konig's not wrong. The longer we wait, the more time they have to tighten their defense."

She turned from them. The woman she'd been, fierce, certain, ready to die for the cause, was fading like the image of Andreas from her mind's eye. In her place was someone else, someone who wanted to live. For Jacob. For the chance to give him a life free of the present darkness.

She could go back to her mother's house, take Jacob, and disappear. Start over somewhere quiet, somewhere safe. She could raise him to be kind, to be good, to never know the weight of his parents' choices. Her mother would help. She'd always been the steady one, the one who'd begged Pavlina to leave this path years ago. Together, they could build something new. Something whole.

"Pavlina," Drewes said softly, pulling her from her thoughts. "What's the plan?"

She opened her eyes. The plan. She didn't have one anymore. Not one she believed in. Her hands trembled, and she clenched them into fists. "I need time," she said, her voice barely above a whisper.

Konig's mouth opened, then closed. Drewes watched her, his expression unreadable. She could feel the weight of their expectations, their trust in her to lead them. But she wasn't sure she could anymore.

"I need to think," she said, softer now. "Alone. Get some rest. Both of you."

The two men hesitated, exchanging a glance, and she saw the flash of a decision between them. They made their move before she had a chance to react.

Konig lunged. He was fast, faster than she'd anticipated in the confined space. Pavlina twisted away, but Drewes was there too, flanking her. She swung at Konig, her fist connecting with his shoulder, but it wasn't enough. He grabbed her arm and twisted it behind her back.

"Stop this!" she snarled, kicking out at Drewes as he closed in. Her boot caught him in the thigh, making him grunt, but he didn't back off. Konig's arm wrapped around her neck from behind, squeezing enough to make her vision blur.

"We don't want to hurt you," Drewes said, his voice strained as he dodged another strike. "But we can't let you ruin this."

Pavlina clawed at Konig's arm, her nails digging into his skin. He cursed, tightening his hold. She stomped down on his foot, feeling the crunch, but he held on. Drewes pulled something from his pocket—a leather sap. She headbutted backward but didn't connect with Konig.

Drewes smacked the sap against the side of her head, and the lights went out.

* * *

Pavlina's body hit the floor hard.

"You said we wouldn't hurt her!" Konig said.

"She'll live." He grinned. "One hell of a headache, though."

They carried her to a corner chair and placed her on the seat. Konig tied her wrists while Drewes tied her ankles. The welt forming on the side of her head from the impact of the sap was turning purple already. She'd be out for a while. A long while.

Drewes and Konig slipped out of the motel room and moved like shadows through the back alley.

They needed wheels. And for what they had planned, using only one car wouldn't cut it. Hitting Ashraf and Mason at the same time was the only way to avoid one alerting the other. They needed two cars.

"Split up," Drewes said as they reached the street. "You take the east lot, I'll hit the west. Something nondescript, nothing flashy."

Konig nodded and hurried off to melt into the night. Drewes headed west. Stealing cars was old hat, but the stakes felt higher now.

The west parking lot was dimly lit. Cars were scattered like forgotten toys. Drewes spotted a gray sedan, older model, no fancy alarms or fuel cutoff systems. Perfect. He approached casually, pulling a slim jim from his jacket. A quick glance around. No one watching. He worked the tool into the door, popping the lock with a soft click.

Inside, he hot-wired it in under a minute, the engine rumbling to life. He pulled out onto the road.

Konig, meanwhile, had better luck in the east lot. A

black SUV caught his eye. Tinted windows, sturdy build. He smashed the window quietly, using his elbow wrapped in his jacket to muffle the noise. He cleared the shards, unlocked the door, and started work under the dash.

Wires sparked, and the SUV growled awake. He grinned. Adrenaline surged. This was what he lived for—the action, the risk.

They met at the side street, engines idling. Drewes rolled down his window. “Any trouble?”

“None,” Konig replied.

“Let’s gear up.”

They grabbed weapons—silenced sub guns and spare ammunition—from their individual rooms and brought them to the vehicles.

Then they drove off in opposite directions.

41

Reema paced in front of Mason's desk with her arms folded and a scowl across her face.

Nathan Mason was tired of watching her.

"I'm as frustrated as you, Reema," he told her.

"I can't believe whoever is after us has vanished."

Despite the strong efforts of Dylan Sharp and his three Eagle operatives, they found no trace of the Faction killers. Nor had there been any further surveillance on either of them. The Faction team had, indeed, seemed to have vanished.

"They may have given up," Mason said. "Alexandra Ruhl is dead. The Faction, what remains, is in tatters."

"No."

"In fact, we should dismiss Dylan and his men."

"*No*, Nathan."

"Reema, the threat is *over*."

"I'm not taking the chance! I'll pay Dylan on my own."

"All right. Will you stop pacing please? We'll give it till

the end of the week when Jack gets back. *Please* settle down."

Reema let out a long breath and stopped but she kept her arms folded and the nasty look on her face.

"You seem upset they haven't tried to kill you," he told her.

"Oh, stop, Nathan. I've had more experienced people than these Faction goons try to kill me, and once they almost succeeded. They're a loose end, and I don't like loose ends. Yes, Ruhl is dead. But if this kill team is running around, they can pull off a revenge hit, somewhere, and come back for us later. And we have no idea where they may be."

"They hide well."

"You only want our bodyguards gone because you're tired of them following you."

Mason laughed. "Following? Gonzales and Matthews are two very capable men who are doing more than following me. They're on me like *shadows*. I can't visit the bathroom without one of them standing within two feet." He pulled back the cuff of his left sleeve to check his watch. "They'll be waiting for us downstairs. Hate to keep our minders waiting. Shall we go?"

Reema followed him out of his office. The night watch crew was taking over the bullpen, others on day watch were leaving at the same time. She grabbed her purse and coat from her office and rode down to the lobby with Mason in a quiet elevator.

"It's either the bodyguards on you every second," she said, "or a bullet in the back, you know."

Mason grunted and remained silent. She had a point

about loose ends, but he didn't think a revenge attack was likely—at least, not in the short term. Faction survivors would be heading underground and undercover for a very long time. The organization might never resurface. Without a leader, the foot soldiers had no resolve or motivation. Unless a new leader emerged from the rubble, Mason figured the Faction was gone for good.

The doors opened on the busy CIA lobby. It was quitting time for most and the start of the day for the night crew. One group of people going out, another coming in. And four men in civilian clothes waiting by the security desk, looking out of place, but part of the scenery. Most people passing by paid them no mind. Dylan Sharp and his men watched the comings and goings, and Sharp raised a hand when he spotted Mason and Reema. Mason and Reema passed through the security exit screen and reached them.

"Does it feel funny being back here, Dylan?" Reema asked.

Dylan Sharp and his trio—Hawk, Matthews, and Gonzales—looked like they were on their way to a sports bar. Casual clothes, light jackets. No weapons. They couldn't get inside carrying weapons. But Mason knew they had plenty of hardware in their vehicles.

"No," Dylan said. "I'm surprised how many have stopped to say hello on their way out."

Mason said, "I'd like to go home now, please."

"Lead the way," Dylan said. "We'll be right behind you."

"Of course you will."

Mason and Reema said goodbye in the parking lot and went to their separate cars. Dylan and Hawk stayed with Reema. Matthews and Gonzales trailed Mason.

Mason walked fast to keep as much distance as possible from Matthews and Gonzales, but it was futile. The two men walked faster to keep up.

* * *

MASON TOOK it easy driving as traffic didn't allow him to go the speed limit. He had to maintain a decent speed to allow Matthews and Gonzales in their blacked-out SUV to keep him in sight. He didn't dislike the two Eagle Alliance men. They were more than capable of handling threats. Obviously well-trained. He had no doubt their ability to run, jump, and shoot matched or even rivaled the best of the best on the Z Section roster. But he didn't appreciate the intrusion into his routine.

He had nothing to hide, of course, other than the fact he had no life outside of work. And it bothered him they might tell somebody—either at their own office, or somebody they knew at CIA...

He had no way to conceal his lifestyle, or lack thereof, from the FBI or CIA's internal security crew who monitored CIA employees to make sure they didn't become a security threat. His routine wasn't unknown to some, but those who knew also kept their mouths shut as part of their responsibilities.

Matthews and Gonzales were under no such obligation.

Then Mason laughed to himself.

What if they don't care?

And if you're so upset about it, get a hobby.

Traffic began to pick up. Mason pressed on the accelerator but glanced back to make sure the SUV stayed close. He might not have liked having them around, but shaking them off wasn't an option. He'd only make their job tougher and have two more people who'd refer to him as the Old Buzzard. Yes, he knew about the whispered nickname. He also didn't care. He was a leader, not a friend. His job description didn't specify being a pal.

But as soon as traffic picked up, brake lights flared once more. Mason slowed. Another glance in the rearview showed the SUV slowing too. Mason sighed and shook his head. Only a couple of more days till Jack returned, and they could call off the watch. Mason had a feeling the days would pass without incident.

* * *

Arno Konig didn't understand why Mason's home lacked a fancy security system. He had no alarm, no sensors on the windows, no security lights in the backyard. Konig parked near the front of Mason's house and then walked around the block to the house behind his. Nobody was home in the second house. He hopped over the fence, traveled through the backyard, and climbed the back fence to Mason's yard. Mason also didn't have a dog. The house sat empty with only a light on in the front entryway.

A glass-cutting tool carved a hole in the rear patio door big enough for Konig to get a hand through and flick the latch. He slid open the door and stepped inside. Taking a knee on the carpet, he grabbed his weapons from the tote bag over his shoulder. He carefully removed the suppressed sub gun, checked the load once more, and then clipped a pair of grenades to his belt. They were high-explosive charges sure to knock down the walls in the close confines of the house. He looked for an ambush position in line with the front door and found the spot at a corner in the kitchen. Time to wait. And fill Mason with lead the second he walked in the door.

42

Mason parked in the driveway and opened the center console. He extracted his Colt Government 1911 .45 automatic and held onto the gun as he climbed out of the car. He had the hammer back and the safety engaged and a round in the chamber, ready for action. Yes, he thought the next few days would pass without incident. He wasn't going to bet his life such an outcome.

Matthews parked the SUV curbside in front of the house. Mason waited for the pair to get out. They carried HK MP5K submachine guns, small enough to hide, but with enough firepower to suppress any threat.

Mason headed up the walk to the front door and used his keys to unlock the bottom knob and the dead bolt. He put the keys away and picked up the briefcase. The .45 went into his waistband for the moment he needed to turn the knob—

"Hold it," Matthews said, stepping in front of him. Matthews held the MP5K in his right hand and turned the knob with his left. The door opened on squeaky hinges.

Gonzales held a small powerful flashlight over their heads and shone the beam into the dark house.

"Clear," he said.

Matthews entered first, turned on a light and echoed Gonzales's statement, then Mason and Gonzales followed. Gonzales shut the door.

"Down!"

Matthews shouted the warning. Mason grabbed for the Colt, but never touched the weapon. Gonzales plowed into him and forced him onto the living room floor. Matthews fired his HK, the crackle of gunfire loud in the room. The whispered snaps of suppressed return fire came from the kitchen. Matthews cried out. The impact of the bullets striking his chest forced him back against the closed door with a thud. He slid to the tiles on the entryway floor and slumped.

Gonzales fired over Mason's body. The ejected shell casings landed on his face. Mason grabbed his gun and clicked off the safety.

"He's in the kitchen!" Gonzales shouted.

"Watch the door by the dining table!" Mason said. It was another way in and out of the kitchen, a swinging door. Gonzales fired again and shouted for Mason to find cover. He ran to another corner ahead. Mason scrambled behind a chair. Not good cover, but enough. And he could see the swinging door on the opposite side of his dining table. Where his late wife hosted many formal dinners. He saw an image of her at the table for a moment, smiling. Her curled hair was swept back, captured with one of the plastic clamps she'd had so many of...

Surrender. Let it happen.

Mason felt a chill as the thought passed through his mind.

But I can't!

The image of his wife faded.

"Hit the deck!" Gonzales shouted, and the man moved fast, seeking cover of his own. The reason became clear in seconds as a grenade sailed down the hall from the kitchen. It bounced off the wall and arced into the living room.

Mason hugged the carpet.

The blast shook the room and windows cracked and broke. Glass cascaded to the floor near him. Mason looked up. He tried to see Gonzales through the smoke. The spot where the grenade detonated was on fire, the orange flames feeding off the carpet fiber. Thick smoke filled the room at a rapid rate.

Gonzales lay still behind another chair. Mason didn't see his entire body, only his legs, but he appeared to lie still.

Let it happen.

Mason choked, coughed, and gripped the .45 tight.

Never. Not like this!

Mason pushed to his feet and covered his mouth. He trained the gun on the swinging door near the dining table as he moved through the smoky room. He reached the corner where Gonzales had been, peeked around. No threat he could see. With the .45 extended in front of him, he slid along the right wall and headed for the kitchen.

He paused. The swinging door opened, he heard the squeak of the hinges, and a burst of gunfire filled the living room. The Faction killer had tried to flank them. He'd have to hunt through the smoke. Mason hurried. He reached the kitchen floor. The swinging door was only ten steps away, and still moving back and forth on its hinges. Mason ran. He was halfway there when the killer came back, pushing the door open with one hand, holding his submachine gun in the other. He was coughing, his eyes tearing from the smoke. Those eyes widened in surprise at the sight of Mason and his Colt .45.

Mason was close enough to ignore the sights, but he lined up front and rear anyway, right on the killer's face. The .45 boomed once, twice. The killer's face sprouted two neat holes as the bullets tore through him. But the slugs tore two chunks out of the back of his head on exit. Blood and bone spattered into the room behind him. The killer collapsed in the doorway, a bundle of arms and legs.

Mason jammed the hot gun in his belt once more and grabbed a red fire extinguisher from the hall closet. Braving the smoky living room once more, he blasted the burning carpet. Fire retardant joined the smoke and created a thick cloud. But the fire went out. Mason dropped the extinguisher and ran back to the kitchen to grab the telephone on the wall. He kept his landline for emergencies such as this, and the call to 9-1-1 connected without delay. He yelled for help, police and medical, and stated there'd been a shooting at his home, and left the phone off the hook.

Back to the hall closet for a first aid kit. But he doubted there was anything he could do for either Matthews or Gonzales.

What about Reema!

He put her out of his mind. Right now, he had to try and save two very brave men who'd taken bullets and a grenade meant for him.

Another thought jolted his pulse rate.

Wait! Where's the cat?

43

Mason oddly hoped the emergency personnel weren't disturbing his neighbors too much.

He sat on the porch steps with a uniformed police officer asking questions. He went through the story as much as he could without divulging any secrets. FBI agents would be on the way, too. A representative from the Agency was also heading to the scene. But Mason wasn't waiting. He knew the limits of what he was allowed to say and what he should keep quiet. As he spoke, he watched the medics at the back of the ambulance. They loaded Matthews and Gonzales into the back. Gonzales was banged up bad from the grenade blast, and Matthews was touch-and-go. Their odds of surviving weren't good. Mason hoped the doctors could keep them alive.

Mason finished his statement and answered some clarifying questions. "I have to go back inside," he added.

"For what?"

"I need to find my wife's cat."

“Not a good idea right now, sir,” the officer said.

“Then come with me.”

“Say again?”

“Come with me if you must.” Mason rose to his feet. “But I need to find my wife’s cat. She’ll—kill me if anything happened.”

Mason entered the house with the officer close behind. He ignored the displeased reaction from the crime scene crew scouring the house. Hell with them, Mason decided. And finding Yukon wasn’t going to be easy. You couldn’t call a cat the same way you called a dog. Mason began by checking his favorite spots, under the couch, anywhere the little bastard might hide. No sign. Mason kept the officer hopping as he raced from room to room, and finally dropped to his knees in the bedroom to look under the bed.

There he was.

Yukon sat in a loaf with wide eyes. He was breathing rapidly.

“Hey there,” Mason said. “Get a little fright? So did I. But it’s okay now. You stay there as long as you need to.”

Mason stood again and smiled at the officer.

“Is he okay?” the cop said.

“Oh, he’s fine. My wife won’t get upset with me this time.”

“Wait till she sees the carpet.”

Mason offered a sad smile. “Well, nothing’s perfect, is it?”

Mason and the officer went back outside.

Now he wondered about Reema.

* * *

She kept checking to see if Dylan was behind her.

Reema felt fine during the long drive on the freeway, but after she took her exit, anxiety took over. Her pulse spiked. She looked from side to side and ahead, scanning for threats. The city streets near the condo always seemed safe and benign. Now they reminded her of the war zone her former home became after the US invasion. *How ridiculous!* Buildings stood. People moved about. People were happy. *This isn't Iraq!* And she still checked the rearview to make sure Dylan's SUV remained behind her. There were no obvious threats, only nighttime traffic, bright lights, pedestrians...

You're going to make yourself crazy!

She stopped for a red light and breathed deep to settle her nerves. No luck.

Her purse sat on the passenger seat. She reached for it, removed the Glock-17 from inside, and placed it on her lap. The rearview showed the comforting shape of the headlamps on Dylan's SUV. At least he and Hawk were behind her. If she had their cover, she didn't have to worry. Right?

Settle down.

I wish Jack was here!

There'd been no word from Jack since his report on the action in Saint-Tropez. She wanted to talk to him. She needed to hear his voice and the reassurance he provided. Alexandra Ruhl was dead. Yes. No doubt. The police recovered her body the day after the shootout. But Reema believed what she told Mason. The loose ends were the main threat now. The kill team would carry out their mission and then fade away.

The light turned green.

The cars ahead of Reema passed through the intersection, and she followed. She looked ahead, then left, then looked right as she reached the middle of the intersection...

Bright LEDs filled the car, and the sound of a racing engine filled her ears and then she screamed.

Metal crunched and glass shattered, and she rocked in the seat to the right with the seat belt biting into her body, then to the left and into the driver's window glass. *Crunch.* Pain flared through her. The airbags exploded, and the other car pushed her into opposing traffic. The bright lights ahead blinded Reema once more. Cars screeched to a halt, other impacts quieter, horns blaring. Reema, hurt, blinded, dizzy, cried out as she tried to process what was happening. Bright lights ahead and to the left. They had her in a giant glaring spotlight, and she couldn't see.

Broken glass from the passenger side windows dripped into the car. The cool night air touched her face. She heard doors open and close. And then automatic gunfire blotted out all thoughts as a surge of adrenaline flooded her.

She reached for her gun, but it was gone, tossed somewhere in the collision...

"No!" she yelled.

She clawed at her seat belt, but her fingers wouldn't move properly.

"Come on!"

* * *

DYLAN AND HAWK didn't need to communicate. Dylan exited first, pistol in hand. The lone driver who struck Reema jumped out and aimed a suppressed submachine gun at her. Dylan fired first but missed. His shot smacked into the killer's car. The shooter pivoted to him and Hawk and fired a burst. Dylan used his car door for cover as the SUV rocked with the hits. The killer turned to run around the other side of his vehicle.

Horns honked, people on the sidewalks screamed. Dylan needed to end the threat and get to Reema fast.

Other way around, champ.

"Cover me!" Dylan shouted.

He ran around the back of the SUV, passed Hawk who fired at the killer's car, and raced to Reema. The killer spotted him. Dylan snapped a shot at him and drove the killer back.

He reached Reema's back fender and stayed low as he moved along the side of the car to the driver's door. He tried the handle; it opened. Reema, panicked, couldn't get her seat belt off. She gave him a dazed look.

* * *

Reema's eyes didn't focus on Dylan's face.

"Dyl...I can't—"

"We gotta go, sweetie!" he yelled. His free hand replaced her clumsy grasp on the seat belt release and pressed the button. He grabbed her, and she put her feet on the ground and then dropped to hands and knees on the dirty pavement. She looked for a way out. Bright gas station on one corner, a dark park on the other. The park. She could hide there.

Dylan pulled at her, telling her to go, run. Now! Reema and weaved around stopped cars. She was almost to the curb when her legs gave out. She stumbled and put her hands out and hit the pavement with a slap.

She froze.

Her head hurt. The fall jarred her whole body. Her vision spun.

Run, Reema!

It wasn't her own voice in her head, but the voice of her late half brother. The last words he said to her before bullets cut him down.

She found the strength to get up again. But she was off balance, her vision tipping, and it felt more like a clumsy stomp than a run. She didn't stop. She reached the other side and dropped behind a tall utility box. And then she made the mistake of looking back.

Hawk, still at the SUV, tried to shoot when the killer showed himself, but Hawk didn't get off a shot in time. A burst from the killer's sub gun stitched through the SUV's metal and took Hawk down. He landed on his back. Dylan fired and struck the killer in the right shoulder. The impact spun the killer around, and he struck the car and slipped down to the pavement.

Dylan turned from Reema's car and ran toward her.

The killer stood up. His right arm hung limp at his side, but he held the sub gun in his left. He raised the weapon and aimed at Dylan's back.

"Dylan!"

The bullets hit the target. Dylan's eyes widened in shock and surprise and his mouth hung open but no cry escaped. He stumbled. Reema screamed. Dylan landed face first and his pistol tumbled from his grasp. The gun bounced across the pavement and stopped at the curb.

Reema ran from the utility box and grabbed the gun. A

Beretta 92FS, the thick grip a familiar feel in her hand. The Faction killer advanced in her direction, moving slowly, but moving. She fired at him. He didn't flinch or react and for sure didn't fall. Her head was so scrambled she couldn't aim. Reema turned and ran into the dark.

44

DREWES IGNORED THE FIRE CONSUMING HIS RIGHT ARM. IT WAS useless, hanging limp, his shoulder wrecked. No matter. He could operate his weapon with his left hand.

The city lights and headlamps of the other cars created a kaleidoscope of brightness and darkness, depending on how his vision reacted to the stimuli. But the lights let him see his target. The woman, running into the park. She'd grabbed a gun from her fallen protector who turned out to be no protector at all. But he didn't think her chances were good. She was hurt, her body still in shock from the crash. It would surprise him if she had the motor skills to fight. He stalked toward her. He moved around the other cars and ignored frightened faces. He was a shark homing on the scent of blood in the middle of the ocean.

Almost there...

He reached the fallen "protector" who was bleeding out on the pavement. He passed by. He didn't want to waste bullets on a man who was already dead.

* * *

GRASS. Wet grass. The sprinklers had sprayed earlier. Reema felt the wetness soaking through her shoes and the cuffs of her slacks.

Then the ground dipped into a slope. She stumbled and tumbled and rolled until the ground leveled. Reema managed to hang onto the gun, but the tumble made her dizzy again. She stayed put and let the world spin in front of her.

Sirens. The wail grew in volume. Help incoming. But how long would it take for the police to find her?

A shadow moved at the edge of the park. A man, walking in her direction.

Reema looked around. A concrete structure lit by small security lights sat thirty yards away. It was solid, sitting on a concrete platform opposite the playground. A restroom facility. She could hide there, but not inside—inside offered nowhere to run. But darkness shrouded the back of the structure. The darkness could conceal her.

She shifted on the wet grass and stood, putting her free arm out in case she fell again. She clutched the gun in her right hand. How many times had Dylan fired? How many cartridges remained? She ran, breathing hard. She crossed a cement path, more grass, then stepped onto the playground's loose tanbark. The restroom lights were closer. Brighter. The glare of the lights framed her figure like a stage spotlight.

Instinct kicked into gear. She dropped and rolled under the steel ramp of a tall slide. As she hit the ground, the Faction killer fired at her. The playground took the punishment. The slugs sparked off metal and chunked into wood.

Back on her feet, Reema shifted to the left. The move put the bulk of the playground between her and the killer. The sirens were at their loudest now. Half the police department must have responded.

Another burst of gunfire sparked off playground equipment. The gunfire would bring the cops, but what if they mistook *her* for the threat?

Reema, panting, reached the restroom building and swung around a corner. Darkness at her back—more grass and trees beyond. Ahead, the approaching killer. She swung back. The killer was moving through the playground. She fired twice, flinching at each explosion of ammunition. The killer fired back. The burst sparked off the wall and spat bits of lead and chips of concrete at her face. Reema screamed and fell. She landed on her right side and lost her grip on the pistol. It tumbled away and stopped two feet from her. Reema cursed. The killer ran at her. Reema dove for the Beretta and grabbed the gun. *You can't miss!* She lifted the pistol, and the spill of light highlighted the killer's form. Reema fired once, twice, then again and again. The rounds connected. Holes sprouted in the killer's chest with bigger holes opening on his back as the bullets passed through. The killer's face twisted in a momentary flash of pain, then went slack, with the rest of his body, and he fell forward. Momentum carried his body further, and he crashed onto the pavement a foot away from Reema. But he lay still.

Reema, gasping, let the Beretta fall from her grasp. She lay down and let her head rest on the hard concrete. The night sky overhead was more peaceful than the crash of guns and spilled blood below. She decided to look up for a while. The police were nearby. She heard their calls to one another as they approached the scene.

She was going to lie still and watch the sky and wait for them to find her.

* * *

PAVLINA RITTER CAME to with a start and a choked scream.

Breathing hard, she looked around. She was still in the motel room. Wrists and ankles bound with zip ties. They'd left her on the scratchy carpet. It was quiet. Konig and Drewes had tied her hands in front of her, so she rolled to the bed and used it as leverage to get to her feet.

She had to hop to get around but reached her kit bag in a corner and grabbed a knife. It took a few tries to slash the zip ties apart, but soon she was free.

This was her chance.

Pavlina hurried to pack only her clothing and the fake travel documents. She found their car still parked outside. The keys were on the dresser. She loaded her suitcase and left the room unlocked. Starting the car, she backed out and screeched the tires leaving the parking lot.

Konig and Drewes could try and finish the mission if they wanted. While they were doing so, she had time to get away. If she could get on a plane before the authorities caught them or killed them, so much the better.

But she had to hurry.

Pavlina drove with purpose but kept to the speed limit. No need for a cop to stop her for driving too fast. She had to keep her mind on the prize. Getting to Zurich. Holding Jacob once again. Putting the war behind her for good.

Like Andreas had wanted.

45

Iva Radler exited the elevator. Her clicking heels joined the lobby commotion indicating the conclusion of another workday.

Anybody observing her face would think she was sad.

And she was. The whirlwind of action culminating in her temporary protective custody ended as fast as it began. Rolf Gerheardt hadn't provided details. He only said, "The threat is over. You may return to your normal life."

She'd laughed at him.

How could life be normal again?

She returned to work and took care of her sister's affairs and funeral arrangements. But the weight of the ordeal remained on her shoulders. She'd carry the weight for a long time.

And she wondered what happened to Jack.

She paused mid-step, locking onto a familiar figure standing, waiting. Her mouth opened in surprise.

Jack.

Alive!

Smiling.

She ran to him and offered an awkward hug thanks to her purse and briefcase, but he returned the squeeze. When they separated, she tried to talk but only gibberish came out.

"Hey, it's okay," Slayton said. "You all right?"

Iva took a deep breath and smiled for the first time since she'd returned to work.

"I'll be okay."

"Um...I wanted to see where Karina's buried. Do you have time?"

"Of course. Let's go."

They rode without talking for a few minutes.

She said, "Is everything...I mean—"

"We got 'em, Iva. All of them."

"I guess that's what I need to know."

"I wish I could tell you more."

"It's a secret. I understand. And I probably don't want any details anyway."

"How's your apartment?"

"All cleaned up. The office has me on light duty for now. The government explained what they could. Gerheardt visited and spoke to my boss himself."

"Rolf is a good man."

The conversation stalled. She let the quiet continue the rest of the way to the cemetery.

Karina Radler had a modest headstone next to her mother and father. Iva stood beside Slayton. They looked at the headstone and Karina's name.

"Can you...excuse me a moment?" Slayton said.

"Sure. I'll go over there."

She moved away and left him alone.

* * *

SLAYTON KNEELED in front of the headstone. He sighed. "I'm sorry we weren't fast enough," he said.

He froze. He'd wanted to say more but talking to a headstone didn't make any sense. Karina was gone. She couldn't hear or respond. She was in the void or wherever one went when life left the body. It was the final mystery. Nobody found the solution until they departed and had no way to report on the experience.

But a part of her still survived in Iva. He decided there was some consolation in the idea. But it didn't make him feel better.

He and Kara tied up the final details in Saint-Tropez and returned to Berlin to complete their individual reports, which went to the Germans and the CIA. He was going home on an evening flight, but didn't want to leave without saying goodbye to Iva. And Karina.

He looked at the headstone some more. There was nothing left to do or say. He'd paid his respects. But he wished he'd been able to do more.

Rising, he rejoined Iva at a nearby tree.

"Got any plans for dinner?" he asked.

"No."

"Let's go eat. Uncle Sam is paying. I'm leaving in a few hours, and I don't want to fly home hungry."

They went back to her car.

* * *

LATER, Kara Botticker drove Slayton to the airport.

"Have a safe trip home," she told him. "Maybe we'll do another job together someday."

"But no more husband-and-wife cover."

"We'll be brother and sister instead."

"More like second cousins three times removed."

She didn't laugh.

Always consistent, he thought.

Slayton grabbed his bag, thanked her for the ride, and left the car. Kara pulled into traffic the second his feet touched the walkway in front of the terminal building.

He wished he was taking a different flight, but Mason promised to meet him at Dulles no matter the time. And for Mason, it would be late indeed.

Nine hours later, the jet touched down at Dulles. Slayton, tired but alert, found Mason waiting at baggage claim. He looked grim. Slayton kept calm. But he knew Mason didn't have good news.

"What happened?" he asked.

"We'll talk in the car."

They did. As Mason drove, he filled Slayton in on every detail of the past twenty-four hours.

Slayton said, "Is Reema—"

"She's all right. Concussion, whiplash, cuts, and bruises. She did well despite her injuries. Your pal Dylan—"

"What happened?"

"He and his men are in bad shape, Jack. They almost didn't make it, and they won't get out of the hospital for a few months. But they'll recover. It was too close."

"Is Reema still in the hospital?"

"She's waiting for you at home."

Tension left Slayton's body. He let out a breath. Reema was safe. Then his concern for Dylan took over. He didn't know the other operatives involved, but said a silent prayer for their recovery, too.

Mason dropped him off at the condo and told him to take two days before coming into the office for debrief and review. Slayton didn't argue.

Reema pulled the door open the moment his key scratched the lock.

She flung her arms around him, and they squeezed each other tight. She wore pajamas with her hair tied back. Somehow, she seemed more fragile in his arms than when he left.

"You should be in bed," he said.

"So take me there."

Slayton locked the door, and Reema slid under the covers while he undressed. He joined her, and they snuggled close. She breathed against his neck, then started to cry. Her tears touched his skin.

"It's all right," he said.

"Dylan almost died, Jack."

"But he didn't."

He held her. He didn't want to talk. Slayton wanted to lie in the dark with Reema and wait for the new day. Everything could wait until the sun rose once more.

* * *

THE CRACK of the baseball bat echoed through the park.

Number Six ran to first base as the ball sailed into the outfield. Three boys on the opposing team tried to catch the ball and failed. Number Six ran to second, then third. One of the three boys in the outfield grabbed the ball and then dropped it. Number Six sprinted for home. By the time the outfielders had the ball, Number Six slid into home plate in cloud of victorious dust.

The parents in the crowd cheered.

Slayton watched from the parking lot. Hank Downing, his buddy killed in the Shipwreck Bar bombing, a bombing orchestrated by Andreas Ritter, would have been proud of his kid even if he'd struck out.

The boy's teammates congratulated him as he returned to the dugout.

Slayton watched the boy's mother. She sat in the bleachers and took pictures of her son. He didn't go any closer because he didn't want to suffer her wrath. He didn't want to see the anger in her eyes or listen to the harsh tone of her words. She didn't want Jack or any of Hank's former SEAL buddies anywhere near her or her son. He had to respect her decision, but he wanted to tell her the man who killed her husband was dead.

Would it matter?

Did any of it matter?

Yes, he decided. It mattered. But he didn't know how to explain why.

He checked his watch. Dylan remained in the hospital, but awake in bed, and was able to receive visitors. He shared a room with his three operatives. Slayton wanted to see Dylan and thank him and his men. He was glad they survived for him to do so.

Slayton watched the kids play a few minutes longer. Hank's kid wasn't going to be up at bat for a little while, but he enjoyed watching the boy's enthusiasm as his teammates went up to bat. His father had shared the same joy.

Slayton checked his watch again.

If he didn't leave soon, the boy's mother might turn and see him.

Slayton didn't want to see her for his own reasons.

He had failed to save her husband. And he had failed to save Karina. They were two more scars joining the ones already marking his body. They remained invisible. Only he knew where those scars resided. And they were permanent.

But he had to live with them.

The game continued. Boys and parents cheered.

Slayton turned and walked away.

AUTHOR'S NOTE

Thank you for reading *Iron Ghost*. I hope you enjoyed reading it as much as I enjoyed writing it! I can't wait for you to read *Jack Slayton #3: Target Package*, which is going to pump up the action even more.

Please visit my website at www.briandrakebooks.com for more book news. You can email me from there; I answer all my mail! You can also listen to my podcast by clicking the PODCAST tab on the home page.

Cordially,
Brian Drake

ABOUT THE AUTHOR

A twenty-five year veteran of radio and television broadcasting, Brian Drake has spent his career in San Francisco where he's filled writing, producing, and reporting duties with stations such as KPIX-TV, KCBS, KQED, among many others. Currently carrying out sports and traffic reporting duties for Bloomberg 960, Brian Drake spends time between reports and carefully guarded morning and evening hours cranking out action/adventure tales.

A love of reading when he was younger inspired him to create his own stories, and he sold his first short story, "The Desperate Minutes," to an obscure webzine when he was 25 (more years ago than he cares to remember, so don't ask).

Brian Drake lives in California with his wife and two cats, and when he's not writing he is usually blasting along the back roads in his Corvette with his wife telling him not to drive so fast, but the engine is so loud he usually can't hear her.

briandrakebooks.com

www.ingramcontent.com/pod-product-compliance
Lightning Source LLC
LaVergne TN
LVHW091114080826
845145LV00008B/1908
* 9 7 8 1 6 8 5 4 9 6 5 7 9 *